# William Shakespeare's King Lear: A Retelling in Prose

David Bruce

Published by David Bruce, 2022.

WILLIAM SHAKESPEARE'S KING LEAR: A RETELLING IN PROSE

**First edition. July 26, 2022.**

Copyright © 2022 David Bruce.

ISBN: 979-8201256357

Written by David Bruce.

# Table of Contents

# Dedication

**Dedicated to Carl Eugene Bruce and Josephine Saturday Bruce**

My father, Carl Eugene Bruce, died on 24 October 2013. He used to work for Ohio Power, and at one time, his job was to shut off the electricity of people who had not paid their bills. He sometimes would find a home with an impoverished mother and some children. Instead of shutting off their electricity, he would tell the mother that she needed to pay her bill or soon her electricity would be shut off. He would write on a form that no one was home when he stopped by because if no one was home he did not have to shut off their electricity.

The best good deed that anyone ever did for my father occurred after a storm that knocked down many power lines. He and other linemen worked long hours and got wet and cold. Their feet were freezing because water got into their boots and soaked their socks. Fortunately, a kind woman gave my father and the other linemen dry socks to wear.

My mother, Josephine Saturday Bruce, died on 14 June 2003. She used to work at a store that sold clothing. One day, an impoverished mother with a baby clothed in rags walked into the store and started shoplifting in an interesting way: The mother took the rags off her baby and dressed the infant in new clothing. My mother knew that this mother could not afford to buy the clothing, but she helped the mother dress her baby and then she watched as the mother walked out of the store without paying.

***

The doing of good deeds is important. As a free person, you can choose to live your life as a good person or as a bad person. To be a good person, do good deeds. To be a bad person, do bad deeds. If you do good deeds, you will become good. If you do bad deeds, you will become bad. To become the person you want to be, act as if you already are that kind of person. Each of us chooses what kind of person we will become. To become a good person, do the things a good person does. To become a bad person, do the things a bad person does. The opportunity to take action to become the kind of person you want to be is yours.

Human beings have free will. According to the Babylonian Niddah 16b, whenever a baby is to be conceived, the Lailah (angel in charge of contraception) takes the drop of semen that will result in the conception and asks God, "Sovereign of the Universe, what is going to be the fate of this drop? Will it develop into a robust or into a weak person? An intelligent or a stupid person? A wealthy or a poor person?" The Lailah asks all these questions, but it does not ask, "Will it develop into a righteous or a wicked person?" The answer to that question lies in the decisions to be freely made by the human being that is the result of the conception.

A Buddhist monk visiting a class wrote this on the chalkboard: "EVERYONE WANTS TO SAVE THE WORLD, BUT NO ONE WANTS TO HELP MOM DO THE DISHES." The students laughed, but the monk then said, "Statistically, it's highly unlikely that any of you will ever have the opportunity to run into a burning orphanage and rescue an infant. But, in the smallest gesture of kindness — a warm smile, holding the door for the person behind you, shoveling the driveway of the elderly person next door — you have committed an act of immeasurable profundity, because to each of us, our life is our universe."

In her book titled *I Have Chosen to Stay and Fight*, comedian Margaret Cho writes, "I believe that we get complimentary snack-size portions of the afterlife, and we all receive them in a different way." For Ms. Cho, many of her snack-size portions of the afterlife come in hip hop music. Other people get different snack-size portions of the afterlife, and we all must be on the lookout for them when they come our way. And perhaps doing good deeds and experiencing good deeds are snack-size portions of the afterlife.

• The Zen master Gisan was taking a bath. The water was too hot, so he asked a student to add some cold water to the bath. The student brought a bucket of cold water, added some cold water to the bath, and then threw the rest of the water on a rocky path. Gisan scolded the student: "Everything can be used. Why did you waste the rest of the water by pouring it on the path? There are some plants nearby which could have used the water. What right do you have to waste even a drop of water?" The student became enlightened and changed his name to Tekisui, which means "Drop of Water."

# Educate Yourself
# Read Like A Wolf Eats
# Be Excellent to Each Other
# Books Then, Books Now, Books Forever

***

In this retelling, as in all my retellings, I have tried to make the work of literature accessible to modern readers who may lack some of the knowledge about mythology, religion, and history that the literary work's contemporary audience had.

Do you know a language other than English? If you do, I give you permission to translate this book, copyright your translation, publish or self-publish it, and keep all the royalties for yourself. (Do give me credit, of course, for the original retelling.)

I would like to see my retellings of classic literature used in schools, so I give permission to the country of Finland (and all other countries) to give copies of this book to all students forever. I also give permission to the state of Texas (and all other states) to give copies of this book to all students forever. I also give permission to all teachers to give copies of this book to all students forever.

Teachers need not actually teach my retellings. Teachers are welcome to give students copies of my eBooks as background material. For example, if they are teaching Homer's *Iliad* and *Odyssey*, teachers are welcome to give students copies of my *Virgil's* Aeneid: *A Retelling in Prose* and tell students, "Here's another ancient epic you may want to read in your spare time."

# CAST OF CHARACTERS

Lear, King of Britain; King Lear is over 80 years old.

King of France.

Duke of Burgundy.

Duke of Cornwall.

Duke of Albany.

Earl of Kent.

Earl of Gloucester (pronounced Gloster).

Edgar, legitimate son to Gloucester.

Edmund, bastard son to Gloucester.

Curan, a courtier.

Oswald, steward to Goneril.

Old Man, tenant to Gloucester.

Doctor.

Fool.

An Officer, employed by Edmund.

A Gentleman, attendant on Cordelia.

A Herald.

Servants to Cornwall.

Goneril, Lear's oldest daughter; married to the Duke of Albany.

Regan, Lear's middle daughter; married to the Duke of Cornwall.

Cordelia, Lear's youngest daughter; at the beginning of the play, she is unmarried.

Knights of Lear's train, Officers, Messengers, Soldiers, and Attendants.

Scene: Britain.

Note: Duke is a title higher than Earl.

# CHAPTER 1
## — 1.1 —

In King Lear's palace, the Earl of Kent, the Earl of Gloucester, and Edmund, who was Gloucester's bastard son, were talking together.

The Earl of Kent said to the Earl of Gloucester, "I thought the King had more preferred the Duke of Albany than the Duke of Cornwall."

The Duke of Albany had recently married King Lear's oldest daughter, Goneril, while the Duke of Cornwall had recently married King Lear's middle daughter, Regan.

The Earl of Gloucester replied, "It always seemed so to us, but now, in the division of the Kingdom, it is not apparent which of the two Dukes he values most. The shares of the Kingdom for the two Dukes are so equally divided that the closest examination of the two shares cannot make either Duke covet the other Duke's share."

"Isn't this your son, my lord?" the Earl of Kent asked the Earl of Gloucester, motioning toward Edmund.

"I have paid for his upbringing," the Earl of Gloucester replied. "I have so often blushed to acknowledge him as my son that now I am inured to it and can brazenly say that he is mine."

"I cannot conceive what you mean," the Earl of Kent replied.

"Sir, this young fellow's mother could very definitely conceive," the Earl of Gloucester punned. "In fact, upon conceiving she grew round-wombed with a pregnant belly, and had, indeed, sir, a son for her cradle before she had a husband for her bed. Do you smell a fault from what I say? Edmund, my son, is illegitimate."

"I cannot wish the fault undone since the issue of it is so handsome," the Earl of Kent diplomatically replied.

"But I also have, sir, a son by order of law — he is legitimate — about a year older than this son. My legitimate son is no dearer to me than my illegitimate son. Though this knave came somewhat saucily into the world before he was sent for, yet his mother was beautiful, there was good entertainment at his making, and the whoreson must be acknowledged."

The Earl of Gloucester called his illegitimate son, Edmund, names such as "knave" and "whoreson," but he used those names affectionately.

He asked his illegitimate son, "Do you know this noble gentleman, Edmund?"

"No, my lord."

"He is my lord of Kent," the Earl of Gloucester said. "Remember him hereafter as my honorable friend."

"I am at your service, my lord," Edmund said respectfully.

"I want to be your friend, and I will do what I can to know you better," the Earl of Kent replied.

"Sir, I shall make every effort to deserve your respect and earn your high opinion."

"Edmund has been out of the country for nine years, and he shall go away again," the Earl of Gloucester said.

Hearing trumpets blow, he added, "The King is coming."

King Lear, the Duke of Cornwall, and the Duke of Albany entered the room. With them were the King's daughters — Goneril, Regan, and Cordelia — and some attendants. One attendant carried a coronet, which someone below the rank of King was meant to wear. Events would show that the person intended to wear the coronet was Cordelia.

King Lear said, "Usher into the royal presence the lords of France and Burgundy, Gloucester."

"I shall, my liege," Gloucester replied and then exited. Edmund went with him.

"In the meantime we shall express our darker purpose," King Lear said, using the royal plural. "This purpose is dark because we have kept it secret from all of you; however, some of you already know part — but only part — of what I am going to do. Give me the map. Know that we have divided into three our Kingdom, and it is our firm intent to shake all cares and responsibilities from our age. As you know, I am over 80 years old. We will confer our cares and responsibilities on younger strengths, while we, unburdened, crawl toward death."

King Lear had talked of his "darker purpose." "Darker" meant "secret" or "hidden," but many of the people listening to him, such as the Earl of Kent, believed that it was a bad idea to divide the Kingdom and that it would have dark and evil consequences.

King Lear continued, "Our son-in-law of Cornwall, and you, our no less loving son-in-law of Albany, pay attention. We have this hour a firm purpose to make known publicly our daughters' individual dowries, so that future strife may be prevented now. Because you will receive your share of the Kingdom before I die, no one needs to fight over his share after I die.

"The King of France and the Duke of Burgundy are great rivals for the love of Cordelia, our youngest daughter, who is still unmarried. Long in our court they have made their amorous sojourn, courting Cordelia. Today, the decision about whom Cordelia will wed will be made.

"Tell me, my daughters — since now we will divest ourself of rule, possession of territory, and the cares of government — which of you shall we say loves us most? I will give the largest dowry to that daughter whose natural affection for her father merits the largest territory.

"Goneril, you are our eldest-born; you will speak first."

"Sir, I love you more than words and language can make clear," Goneril said. "To me you are dearer than eyesight, possession of land, and freedom of action. You are beyond what can be valued as rich or rare. I love you no less than I love life with grace, health, beauty, and honor. I love you as much as a child has ever loved, or a father has ever found himself to be loved. My love for you is a love that makes language poor, and speech inadequate to express how much I love you."

Cordelia was disgusted by the fulsomeness of Goneril's praise, and she expected to hear the same kind of praise from her other sister, Regan. By pouring on the praise, these two sisters hoped to benefit by receiving bigger dowries.

Cordelia also worried. She thought, *What should Cordelia do? Love, and be silent.*

Cordelia loved her father, but she loathed fulsome praise that was used to manipulate a father in order to gain wealth. It is better to show one's love though one's actions rather than fake it through one's words.

King Lear pointed to the map and said to Goneril, "Of all these boundaries, even from this line to this, with shady forests and with enriched open plains with plenteous rivers and extensive meadows, we make you lady. This territory will perpetually belong to your and Albany's descendants."

He then said, "What does our second daughter, our dearest Regan, wife to Cornwall, have to say? Speak."

Regan replied, "Sir, I am made of the self-same mettle that my sister is. Prize me at her worth. Value me as you value her."

"Mettle" meant "nature" or "character." However, it is a homonym for "metal." Subsequent events would show that both Goneril and Regan were hard-hearted.

Regan continued, "In my true heart I find that Goneril names what my love really is — only she comes too short. I profess that I am an enemy to all other joys that the most perfect part of me can enjoy, and I find that I am made happy only in your dear Highness' love."

Regan's quest for a bigger dowry had caused her to be even more fulsome in her description of her love for her father than her older sister, Goneril. If Regan, as she had said, really is made happy only in the love of her father, then loving her husband and being loved by him brings her no happiness.

Cordelia thought, *Poor Cordelia! And yet I am not so, since I am sure that my love for my father is richer than my tongue. I love my father more than I can say.*

Pointing to the map, King Lear said to Regan, "To you and your descendants forever after will belong this ample third of our fair Kingdom. It is no less in space, value, and pleasure than that conferred on Goneril."

He then turned to Cordelia and said, "Now, our joy, although you are the last of my daughters to be born and therefore the youngest, the King of France with its vineyards and the Duke of Burgundy with its dairy pastures strive for your love and wish to marry you. What can you say to draw a third of the Kingdom that is more opulent than your sisters' shares?"

King Lear had planned from the beginning to give Cordelia a better part of the Kingdom than he would give to her sisters. Her sisters were already married, and an excellent dowry would help Cordelia to get an excellent husband. Besides, Cordelia was his favorite daughter. One of several reasons to divide up the Kingdom now — before he died — was to give Cordelia the best share. If the Kingdom were divided after his death, Cordelia, being the youngest, would get the worst share, or no share.

Cordelia remained silent, so King Lear told her, "Speak. What can you say to draw a third of the Kingdom that is more opulent than your sisters' shares?"

She gave an honest, not a fulsome, answer: "Nothing, my lord."

Shocked, King Lear exclaimed, "Nothing!"

"Nothing," Cordelia repeated.

"Nothing will come from nothing," King Lear said. "Speak again."

"Unhappy that I am, I cannot heave my heart into my mouth," Cordelia said.

Ecclesiasticus 21:26 states, "*The heart of fools is in their mouth: but the mouth of the wise is in their heart.*"

Cordelia continued, "I love your majesty according to my filial duty — no more and no less. I love you as a daughter ought to love her father."

"Cordelia! Mend your speech a little, or it may mar your fortunes."

"My good lord," Cordelia said, "you have begotten me, bred me, and loved me. I return those duties back to you as are rightly fit. I obey you, love you, and greatly honor you.

"Why do my sisters have husbands, if they say that all their love is for you? When I shall wed, that lord who takes my hand shall carry half my love with him, as well as half my care and duty. Half of my love will be for you, and half will be for my husband. To be sure, I shall never marry like my sisters have; they give you all their love and none to their husband."

"Do you say this from your heart?" King Lear asked.

"Yes, my good lord."

"Can you be so young, and so untender? Are you really this hard-hearted?"

"I am so young, my lord, and I say the truth. I am honest."

"Let it be so," King Lear said. "Your truth, then, shall be your dowry. I swear by the sacred radiance of the Sun, the mysteries of the underworld goddess Hecate, and the night; by all the operations of the astrological orbs from whom we exist, and cease to be, that here I disclaim all my paternal care, kinship, and common blood with you. From here on, I regard you as a stranger to my heart and me, forever. The barbarous Scythian, or that person who cannibalizes his parents and children to feed his appetite, shall to my bosom be as well neighbored, pitied, and relieved as you, my former daughter. I renounce you; you are no longer my daughter. You are no kin of mine."

The Earl of Kent began to object: "My good liege —"

King Lear shouted, "Peace, Kent! Silence! Come not between the dragon and his wrath. I loved Cordelia the most, and I thought to give all the rest I had to her in return for her tender loving care. Leave, and avoid my sight!"

The Earl of Kent did not leave.

King Lear said, "Now it seems that I will find my peace in my grave, as here I take her father's heart away from her and give it away to someone else!"

He ordered, "Call the King of France!"

Everyone was stunned; no one moved.

King Lear said, "Who will carry out my orders? Call the Duke of Burgundy, too."

Some attendants left.

Pointing to the map, King Lear said, "Cornwall and Albany with my two daughters' dowries digest this third dowry — the one that should have been Cordelia's. Let pride, which Cordelia calls plain-speaking, be her dowry and get her a husband. I do invest you, Cornwall and Albany, jointly with my power, first position, and all the magnificent trappings that accompany majesty.

"We reserve for ourself a hundred Knights, by you to be paid. We shall also reside with you, by turn, one month at a time. We retain for ourself the title of King, and all the honors and prerogatives that are due to a King. You two shall have the power and authority, revenue, and execution of the royal duties and responsibilities. Beloved sons-in-law, they are yours. To confirm what I say, share this coronet between yourselves."

The Earl of Kent said, "Royal Lear, whom I have ever honored as my King, loved as my father, followed as my master, and mentioned in my prayers as my great patron —"

King Lear warned the Earl of Kent, "The bow is bent and drawn; stay out of the way of the arrow."

The Earl of Kent replied, "Let the arrow fly even though the forked arrowhead invades the region of my heart. Kent shall be without manners when Lear is mad. What will you do, old man? Do you think that I will ignore my duty and be afraid to speak up when a powerful man bows down before flattery? An honorable man is bound by duty to speak out when majesty stoops to folly. Reverse your judgment; change your decision, and after you have thought things over carefully, stop this hideous rashness. I will stake my life that what I say is true: Your youngest daughter does not love you least, nor are those empty-hearted whose low sound reverbs no hollowness. Cordelia may not be able to fulsomely express how much she loves you, but she loves you nonetheless. My duty is to speak truth to power."

"Kent, on your life, speak no more," King Lear threatened.

"My life I have never valued except as a pawn to wage war against your enemies, nor am I afraid to lose it in an attempt to keep you safe."

"Get out of my sight!" King Lear shouted.

"See better, Lear," the Earl of Kent said, "and aim your sight at me. I will not lead you astray."

King Lear started to speak: "Now, by Apollo —"

"Now, by Apollo, King," the Earl of Kent interrupted, "you swear by your gods in vain."

"Oh, vassal! Unbeliever!" King Lear shouted, laying his hand on his sword.

Both the Duke of Albany and the Duke of Cornwall said to King Lear, "Dear sir, don't."

The Earl of Kent said to King Lear, "Do. Kill your physician, and give the physician's fee to your foul disease. Revoke your decision. Or, if you do not, as long as I can shout from my throat, I'll tell you that you are making a mistake and are doing evil."

"Hear me, traitor!" King Lear shouted. "On your allegiance, hear me! Since you have sought to make us break our vow, something that we have never dared to do, and since with unnatural pride you have intervened between our order and its carrying out, something that neither our nature nor our high position as King can bear, I now demonstrate my power and give you your reward for your interference. We allow you five days to get provisions to shield yourself from the disasters and evils of the world. On the sixth day, you must turn your hated back upon our Kingdom. If, on the tenth day following, your banished body is found in our dominions, that moment will be the moment you die. Get out! By Jupiter, we shall never revoke your exile!"

"Fare you well, King," the Earl of Kent said. "Since thus you will appear, freedom lives out of your country, and banishment is here."

He said to Cordelia, "The gods to their dear shelter take you, maiden, who justly think, and have most rightly said!"

He said to Regan and Goneril, "And I hope that your deeds may show that your large and generous speeches were true, so that good effects may spring from words of love."

He said to the Duke of Albany and the Duke of Cornwall, "Thus Kent bids all you Princes *adieu*; he'll shape his old course in a country new. I will stay true to myself — and speak the truth — in another country."

The Earl of Kent exited.

The Earl of Gloucester returned to the presence of King Lear. With him were the King of France, the Duke of Burgundy, and some attendants.

The Earl of Gloucester said, "Here are the King of France and the Duke of Burgundy, my noble lord."

"My lord of Burgundy," King Lear said, "we first address ourself to you, who with this King of France have been competing to marry Cordelia, our daughter. What is the least dowry that you would require to be paid immediately to marry my daughter, without which you would cease your quest of love?"

"Most royal majesty, I crave no more than what your Highness has already offered, and I am sure that you will not offer less."

"Right noble Burgundy, when Cordelia was dearly beloved by us, we did regard her as being dear and valuable, but now her price has fallen. Sir, there she stands. If you like anything within her, who seems to be worth little, or if you like all of her, she is there, and she is yours. But be aware that I am displeased with her, and I will not give her a dowry. If you want to marry her without a dowry, then marry her. If you must receive a dowry in order to marry her, then do not marry her."

"I don't know what to say," the Duke of Burgundy replied.

"Will you marry Cordelia although she possesses infirmities and imperfections, although she lacks friends, although she has recently earned our hatred, although her only dowry is our curse upon her head, and although I have sworn that she is no longer my daughter? Will you take her, or leave her?"

"Pardon me, royal sir," the Duke of Burgundy said. "No choice can be made when such conditions exist. A true choice involves two viable options to choose between. Here only one viable option exists to be chosen."

"Then leave her, sir," King Lear said. "You have good reason — by the power who made me, I have told you all her wealth."

King Lear then said, "As for you, great King of France, I have such friendship for you that I would not do anything to harm it such as have you marry a female I hate; therefore, I advise you to cease loving Cordelia. Instead, avert your liking to a worthier maiden. Do not love a wretch whom Nature is almost ashamed to acknowledge hers. Cordelia is unnatural."

"This is very strange," the King of France said. "Cordelia very recently was the main object of your love, the subject of your praise, the balm of your age. How can the best and dearest Cordelia in a moment of time commit an action so monstrous that it dismantles so many layers of your favor? Surely, her offense must be so unnatural that it is monstrous, or else the affection you previously felt for her was undeserved — but it would take a miracle for me to believe either of these things."

Cordelia said to King Lear, "I beg your Majesty — even though I lack the ability to do what the glib and oily do, which is to speak and promise to do something without meaning to do what they say and promise; in contrast, when I intend to do something, I do it before I speak — that you make known that it is no vicious blot such as murder or other foul immorality, no unchaste action or dishonorable action, that has deprived me of your grace and favor. What has done that is the lack of things that I am richer for not having: an always-begging eye and such a fulsome tongue as I am glad I do not have, although not to have it has deprived me of your like for me."

Cordelia deliberately chose to use the word "like" instead of "love."

King Lear replied, "It would have been better for you never to have been born than to have failed to please me better."

The King of France asked, "Is Cordelia's fault only this — a natural tendency not to announce publicly what she intends to do?"

He asked, "My lord of Burgundy, what do you say to the lady? Love's not love when it is mingled with regards that stand aloof from the entire point. Love ought not to be affected by a dowry or the lack of a dowry. Will you have her? She is herself a dowry. Will you marry Cordelia?"

"Royal Lear," the Duke of Burgundy said, "if you give as her dowry that portion which you yourself proposed, then I will take Cordelia by the hand and make her Duchess of Burgundy."

"I will give nothing as her dowry," King Lear replied. "I have sworn that. I am firm in my decision and will do what I have sworn to do."

The Duke of Burgundy said to Cordelia, "I am sorry, then. You have lost a father, and now you must lose a husband."

Cordelia said, "May peace be with Burgundy! Since he loves status and money, I shall not be his wife."

The King of France said, "Fairest Cordelia, you are most rich, being poor; most choice, being forsaken; and most loved, being despised! Here and now I seize upon you and your virtues. It is lawful for me to take what has been cast away.

"Gods, gods! It is strange that from their cold neglect my love should kindle to inflamed respect. Although the gods neglect you, I even more strongly love you. Your dowerless daughter, King Lear, thrown to my lot, is to be Queen of us, of what is ours, and of our fair France. Not all the Dukes of waterish Burgundy can buy this unprized precious maiden away from me."

By "waterish Burgundy," the King of France meant that the Duke of Burgundy was weak. Blood did not flow in his veins — only weak water did.

The King of France added, "Bid them farewell, Cordelia, although they have been unkind to you. What you lose here, you will find better elsewhere."

"You have her, King of France," King Lear said. "Let her be yours, for we have no such daughter, nor shall we ever see that face of hers again. Therefore, Cordelia, be gone without our grace, our love, or our benison and blessing. Come, noble Duke of Burgundy."

Everyone left except the King of France, Goneril, Regan, and Cordelia.

The King of France said to Cordelia, "Bid farewell to your sisters."

Cordelia said, "With eyes washed by tears, Cordelia leaves you, the jewels of our father. I know you for what you really are, and like a sister I am very loath to call your faults by their actual names. Treat our father well. To your professed bosoms I commit him, but if I still were within his grace, I would recommend him to a better place. So, farewell to you both."

Cordelia had committed her father to her sisters' "professed bosoms" — the love that they had professed for him, aka the love that they had said that they had for him. She wanted them to treat him with all the love that they had publicly proclaimed that they had for him. She did not want them to treat him the way that they actually felt about him.

"Don't tell us what our duty to our father is," Regan said.

"Concern yourself with making your husband happy," Goneril said. "He is the one who is marrying you as an act of charity. You have failed in your obedience as a daughter, and you well deserve to be treated by your husband with the same lack of love that you have shown to your father."

"Time shall unfold what covered cunning hides," Cordelia said. "Time at first covers faults, but eventually it reveals and derides them. Well may you prosper!"

"Come, my fair Cordelia," the King of France said.

He and Cordelia exited.

Goneril said to Regan, "Sister, I have to talk to you about something that closely concerns us both. I think our father will depart from here tonight."

"That's very certain," Regan said. "He will leave and stay with you; next month he will stay with us."

"You see how full of changes he is in his old age," Goneril said. "We have seen much evidence of those changes. He always loved our sister most; it is grossly obvious that he used poor judgment when he cast her off."

"It is the infirmity of his old age," Regan said, "yet he has always known himself only but little."

"He was rash even when he was at his best and soundest," Goneril said. "What can we look forward to now that he is old? He will have the imperfections that he has always had, but added to them will be the unruly waywardness that unhealthy and angry old age bring with them."

"He is likely to continue to engage in such impulsive outbursts as that which led to Kent's banishment," Regan said. "That is the behavior that we are likely to see our father engaging in."

"There will be additional formalities before the King of France leaves here," Goneril said. "Please, let's sit and put our heads together. If our father continues to exert authority with his customary impulsiveness, then his recent abdication of his power to us will be in name only — he will be a problem to us."

"We shall think further about it," Regan said.

"We must *do* something," Goneril said. "A blacksmith must strike and shape iron while it is hot or he will lose his labor and opportunity. Like a blacksmith, we also must strike while the iron is hot."

Holding a letter while alone in a room in the Earl of Gloucester's castle, Edmund said to himself, "You, Nature, are my goddess; to your law my services are bound. The laws of Nature are better than the laws of Civilization. Why should I stand in the midst of pestilential customs and permit the finely and curiously detailed laws of nations to deprive me of what I want just because I am some twelve or fourteen months younger than Edgar, my brother.

"Why am I a bastard? Why am I therefore regarded as base? My proportions are as well put together, my mind as noble and refined, and my appearance as like my father's as is Edgar's, who is the son of my father's wife. Why do they brand people like me with the words 'base,' 'baseness,' and 'bastardy'? They call me base, but am I base?

"I am a person who, having been created as the result of lusty stolen natural pleasure, aka adultery, has acquired more beneficial qualities, which are both physical and mental as well as energetic, than a whole tribe of fools who were created in a dull, stale, tired bed — the result of a long marriage — in between bedtime and morning.

"Well, then, legitimate Edgar, I must have your land and other inheritance. Our father's love is the same for the bastard Edmund and for the legitimate Edgar — that's a fine word: 'legitimate'!

"Well, my legitimate Edgar, if this letter I have forged succeeds, and if my plot thrives, Edmund the base shall overtop and surpass Edgar the legitimate.

"I grow; I prosper. Now, gods, stand up for bastards!"

The Earl of Gloucester entered the room. Upset by recent events, he talked to himself.

"Kent has thus been banished! And the angry King of France has departed! And King Lear left last night! He has limited his power! He is now confined to an allowance! All this was done suddenly, as if he had been pricked by a gad — a spear!"

Seeing his illegitimate son and the letter his son was holding, he said, "Edmund, how are you? What is the news?"

"If it please your lordship, there is no news."

He hastily put away the letter he had forged — and looked as if he had a secret reason for putting it out of sight.

"Why are you so eager to put away that letter?" the Earl of Gloucester asked.

"I know no news, my lord," Edmund replied.

"What letter were you reading?"

"I was reading nothing, my lord."

"No?" the Earl of Gloucester said. "Why then did you need to put it in your pocket with such a terrible display of haste? By definition, nothing has no need to hide itself. Let me see it. Come, if it really is nothing, I shall not need spectacles to read it because it is nothing rather than something."

"Please, sir, pardon me," Edmund said. "It is a letter from my brother, and I have not read it all, but judging from the part that I have read, I find it not fit for you to read."

His curiosity aroused, the Earl of Gloucester said, "Give me the letter, sir."

"I shall offend, I see, whether I keep it or give it to you to read. The content of the letter, judging from the part I read, is offensive."

"Let me see it! Let me see it!"

"I hope, for my brother's sake, that he wrote this letter only as a trial or test of my virtue," Edmund said.

The Earl of Gloucester read the letter out loud:

"*This policy of reverence for old age makes bitter the best years of our lives, keeps our fortunes from us until our own old age cannot relish and enjoy our fortunes. I begin to find useless and foolish bondage in the oppression made by aged tyranny, which holds command over us, not because it has power, but because we allow it to. Come to me so that I may speak more about this. If our father would sleep until I waked him, you would enjoy half of his income forever, and live the beloved of your brother, EDGAR.*"

The Earl of Gloucester said, "Ha! This is conspiracy! He wrote about my death: '*If our father would sleep until I waked him, you would enjoy half of his income.*' My son Edgar! Did he write this? Does he have the heart and brain that this thought bred in?"

The Earl of Gloucester said to Edmund, "When did you get this letter? Who brought it to you?"

"It was not brought to me, my lord," Edmund said. "There's the cunning of it. I found this letter in my bedroom — it had been thrown through the window."

"Do you know whether the handwriting is your brother's?"

"If the content of the letter were good, my lord, I would swear that it was his handwriting, but because of the content, I would prefer that the handwriting were not his."

"It is his handwriting," the Earl of Gloucester said.

"True, my lord," Edmund said. "It is his handwriting, but I hope his heart is not in the content."

"Has he ever before tried to find out what you think about this business of taking my income and making me a ward?"

"Never, my lord, but I have heard him often maintain that it is fitting that, when sons are at a mature age, and fathers are declining, the father should be a ward to the son, and the son should manage the father's income."

"Oh, he is a villain — a villain! This is the same opinion that he expressed in the letter! He is an abhorrent villain! He is an unnatural, detestable, brutish villain! He is worse than brutish! Go and find him. I'll arrest him — that abominable villain! Where is he?"

"I do not know for certain, my lord," Edmund said. "If it shall please you to suspend your indignation against my brother until you can get from him better testimony and evidence of his intent, you shall run a safe course; whereas, if you violently proceed against him, mistaking his purpose, it would make a great gap in your own honor, and shake into pieces the heart of his obedience. I dare bet my life that he wrote this letter to test my affection for you, and that he had no more dangerous intention than that."

"Do you really think so?" the Earl of Gloucester asked.

"If your honor judges it fitting, I will place you where you shall hear us talk about this, and with your own ears you shall learn for yourself what his intention was in writing the letter. This can be done without any further delay — we can do it this evening."

"He cannot be such a monster —"

"I am sure that he is not," Edmund said.

"— to his father, who so tenderly and entirely loves him. Heaven and Earth! Edmund, seek him out. Find him, and worm yourself into his confidence for me, please. Find a way — whatever way you think is best — to do this. I would give anything — including my own wealth and rank — to know the truth."

"I will look for him, sir, immediately," Edmund said. "I will carry out the business as I shall find means and let you know what I find out."

"These recent eclipses of the Sun and Moon portend no good to us," the Earl of Gloucester said. "Although human reason can explain these recent eclipses in various ways, yet all of Humankind finds itself scourged by the devastating consequences that follow the eclipses: Love cools, friendship falls off and declines, brothers divide, mutinies and riots occur in cities, discord occurs in countries; treason occurs in palaces, and the bond between son and father is cracked. This villain of mine — Edgar — comes under this prediction: the son goes against the father, the King falls away from his natural temperament, and the father goes against the child.

"We have already seen the best years. Now machinations, emptiness, treachery, and all ruinous disorders follow us disquietly and disturbingly to our graves.

"Edmund, find this villain — Edgar! You shall lose nothing by it; do it carefully.

"And the noble and true-hearted Kent has been banished! What is his offense? It is honesty! Strange!"

The Earl of Gloucester exited.

Alone, Edmund said to himself, "This is the excellent foolishness of the world, that, when bad things happen to us — which are often due to the excesses of our own behavior — we avoid taking responsibility. Instead, we regard the Sun, the Moon, and the stars as guilty of causing our disasters. We think that we were villains by necessity; fools by the compulsion of astrological stars; knaves, thieves, and traitors because of the predominance of astrological planets; drunkards, liars, and adulterers because of an enforced obedience to astrological planetary influence; and all that we are evil in we say was caused by supernatural astrological compulsion.

"What an admirable evasion of responsibility is made by a lecherous man when he says that a star caused his lusty disposition! My father had sexual intercourse with my mother under the Dragon's Tail — the constellation called Drago. And my nativity took place under Ursa Major — the constellation called the Big Bear, in which Mars is predominant but in which Venus has influence. According to astrology, it follows that I am warlike and lecherous."

He thrust his tongue between his lips and blew a raspberry, and then he added, "I would have been what I am even if the maidenliest star in the Heavens had twinkled on my bastardizing. Edgar —"

At this moment, Edgar entered the room.

"— and right on cue here he comes like the conclusion of an old comedy. Now I need to act with villainous melancholy, and heave a sigh like Tom o'Bedlam — an insane beggar — would."

He said more loudly, so that Edgar would hear him, "Oh, these eclipses predict divisions and conflicts!"

Then he hummed to himself and pretended that he did not know that Edgar had entered the room.

"How are you, brother Edmund?" Edgar asked. "What serious contemplation are you engaged in?"

"I am thinking, brother, of a prediction I read the other day about what will follow these eclipses."

"Do you concern yourself about that? Is that really something you want to waste your time on?"

"I promise you that the astrologer writes of very bad consequences, such as unkindness between the child and the parent; death, dearth, dissolutions of friendships that have lasted a long time; divisions in state, as well as menaces and maledictions against King and nobles; needless suspicions and distrusts, banishment of friends, loss of supporters, breaking up of marriages, and I don't know what else."

"How long have you been a devotee of astrology?"

"Come, come; when did you last see my father?"

"Why, just last night."

"Did you speak with him?" Edmund asked.

"Yes, for two hours."

"Did you part on good terms? Did you notice any displeasure in him by his words or in his countenance?"

"None at all," Edgar replied.

"Think about how you may have offended him, and at my entreaty please stay away from him until some time has passed and lessened the heat of his displeasure, which right now so rages in him that his doing physical harm to you would not stop his anger."

"Some villain has done me wrong and has been spreading malicious lies about me," Edgar said.

"I think that you are right," Edmund said. "Please, stay away from him and keep your emotions under control until the intensity of his rage lessens. Also, I ask you to go with me to my quarters, from whence I will bring you at the appropriate time to hear my lord speak. Please, go now. Here's my key. If you need to be outside my quarters, go armed."

"Armed, brother!" Edgar said, astonished.

"Brother, I advise you the best I know how. Arm yourself. Carry weapons. I am not an honest man if I know of any good intention toward you right now. I have told you what I have seen and heard, but only faintly. I have told you nothing like the horrible reality of our father's anger toward you. Please, go now."

"Shall I hear from you soon?"

"I will do what I can to help you."

Edgar exited, and Edmund said to himself, "I have a credulous father! And I have a noble brother, whose nature is so far from doing anyone harm that he thinks that no one would do him harm. On his foolish and honest nature my deceptions work well! I see the treachery ahead of me that I need to do. Let me, if not by birth, have lands by wit. All with me is meet that I can fashion fit. If I cannot get lands through inheritance, I will get them through treachery. I am willing to do whatever it takes."

King Lear was now staying with Goneril in the palace of her husband, the Duke of Albany. In a room of the palace, Goneril was talking to her steward, Oswald.

"Did my father strike my gentleman because he scolded his Fool — his court jester?" Goneril asked.

"Yes, madam."

"By day and night he wrongs me; every hour he bursts out into one gross offense or other that sets us all at odds and throws us into tumult. I'll not endure it. His Knights grow riotous, and he himself upbraids us about every trifle. When he returns from hunting, I will not speak with him; tell him that I am sick. If you slack off your former services to him, you shall do what I want you to do. I will take responsibility for your slothful service to him."

"He's coming, madam," Oswald said. "I hear him."

Horns sounded.

"Be as casually disobedient to him as you please — you and your fellow servants," Goneril said. "I want this to come up for discussion. If he dislikes the servants' behavior, let him go to my sister, whose mind and mine, I know, are in agreement that we will not be ruled by him. He is a foolish and idle old man, who still wants to exert the authority that he has given away! Now, by my life, old fools are babes again; and they must be treated with rebukes in place of flatteries — when they abuse those flatteries. Remember what I tell you."

"I will, madam."

"And let his Knights have colder looks from you and the other servants. The consequences that develop from it do not matter. Tell the other servants that. I want to cause a confrontation so that I can tell my father what I think. I'll write immediately to my sister to tell her to do the same things that I am doing.

"Go, and prepare for dinner."

In a hall in the castle of the Duke of Albany and his wife, Goneril, Kent stood. He was in disguise.

He said to himself, "If I can disguise my voice with an accent, I may succeed in that purpose for which I razed my likeness by, for example, taking a razor to my beard. Now, banished Kent, if you can serve where you stand condemned, it may happen that your master, whom you respect, shall find you working hard to help him."

Some horns sounded, announcing that King Lear had returned from his hunt. King Lear, his Knights, and some attendants entered the hall.

"Let me not wait even a moment for dinner; go and get it ready," King Lear ordered.

An attendant exited.

Seeing the disguised Kent, King Lear asked, "How are you? And what are you?"

"A man, sir."

"What do you profess? What do you want from us?" King Lear asked.

By "profess," King Lear meant "profession" or "special calling," but the disguised Kent interpreted it as meaning "claim."

He said, "I profess to be no less than I seem. I will serve the man truly who will put me in trust, I will respect a man who is honest, I will converse and keep company with a man who is wise and says little, I will fear the judgment of my god, I will fight when I cannot avoid fighting, and I will eat no fish."

By "eat no fish," the disguised Kent meant that he was a Protestant and so did not have to eat fish on Friday, that he was a meat-eater and so a hearty man, and that he did not consort with prostitutes, aka "fish."

"Who are you?" King Lear asked.

"A very honest-hearted fellow, and as poor as the King," the disguised Kent replied.

He took a chance in making that particular joke. King Lear had given his wealth to his two oldest daughters, and he was poor, especially for a King, but he took the joke well, replying, "If you are as poor for a subject as he is for a King, you are poor enough. What do you want?"

"Service," the disguised Kent said. "I want a job."

"Who would you serve?"

"You."

"Do you know me, fellow?"

"No, sir, but you have something in your countenance that makes me want to call you my master."

"What's that?"

"Authority."

"What services can you do?" King Lear asked.

"I can keep an ethical secret, ride, run, mar an excellent tale when I tell it, and deliver a plain message bluntly. I can speak plainly, but do not expect me to speak like a courtier. That which ordinary men are fit for, I am qualified in, and my best quality is diligence."

"How old are you?"

"I am not so young, sir, as to love a woman for singing, nor so old as to dote on her for anything. The years on my back number forty-eight," the disguised Kent said.

"Follow me; you shall serve me," King Lear said. "If I like you no worse after dinner, I will not part from you yet. You will stay in my employ for a while at least."

He then called, "Dinner, ho, dinner! I ordered my dinner a while ago! Where's my knave? My Fool? Go, one of you, and call my Fool hither."

An attendant exited.

Oswald, who was loyal to Goneril, entered the hall.

King Lear said, "You, you, fellow, where's my daughter?"

Oswald said, "Excuse me, sir," and exited without answering King Lear's question. This was no way to treat a King.

Perturbed, King Lear said, "What did the fellow there say to me? Call the blockhead back."

A Knight left to get Oswald.

"Where's my Fool?" King Lear shouted. "I think the world's asleep."

The Knight returned.

"Where's that mongrel?" King Lear asked, referring to Oswald.

"He says, my lord, that your daughter is not well," the Knight said.

"Why didn't the slave come back to me when I called him?"

"Sir, he answered me in the rudest manner that he would not."

"He would not!"

"My lord, I don't know what the matter is, but in my opinion, your Highness is not being treated with that ceremonious affection that used to be shown to you," the Knight said. "I have noticed that a great lessening of kindness appears in the servants in general as well as in the Duke himself and your daughter."

"Do you really think so?" King Lear asked.

The Knight replied, "Please, pardon me, my lord, if I am mistaken. My duty is to speak up when I think your Highness has been wronged."

"You have simply reminded me of what I myself have thought. I have perceived a very faint neglect recently, which I have rather blamed on my own possible over-scrupulousness about how I am treated rather than a deliberate intent on their part to be unkind to me. I will look further into it. But where's my Fool? I have not seen him these two days."

"Since the young lady Cordelia has gone to France, sir, the Fool has much grieved."

"Tell me no more about that," King Lear said. "I have noted it well."

He ordered an attendant, "Go and tell my daughter I want to speak to her."

The attendant exited.

King Lear ordered another attendant, "Tell my Fool to come here."

The attendant exited.

Oswald reentered the hall.

King Lear said to him angrily, "Come here, sir. Who am I, sir?"

"My lady's father," Oswald replied.

Wrong answer.

"'My lady's father'! That's like calling me 'my lord's knave'! You misbegotten dog! You slave! You cur!"

"Begging your pardon, I am none of these things, my lord," Oswald said, staring King Lear in the face.

He was treating King Lear as an equal.

"Do you bandy looks with me, you rascal?" King Lear said, hitting him.

"I'll not be hit, my lord," Oswald said.

"Nor tripped neither, you base football player," Kent said, tripping him.

In this society, members of the upper class played tennis and bandied the ball back and forth, while members of the lower class played football, aka soccer.

"I thank you, fellow," King Lear said to the disguised Kent. "You serve me well, and I'll treat you well."

The disguised Kent yelled at Oswald, "Come, sir, get up and go away! I'll teach you to recognize differences in rank! Get out! Get out! If you want to be thrown on the floor again so you can measure your clumsy length again, stay for a moment, but it will go better for you if you leave! Wise up, and get out of here!"

The disguised Kent threw Oswald out of the hall.

King Lear said, "Now, my friendly fellow, I thank you. Here is a down payment on the money you will earn by being in my service."

The Fool entered the hall as King Lear gave the disguised Kent some money.

A Fool is not a fool. Many Fools are quite wise.

The Fool said, "Let me hire him, too. Here's my coxcomb."

The Fool offered the disguised Kent his Fool's hat, which was designed to look like the coxcomb of a rooster.

"How are you, my fine fellow?" King Lear asked his Fool.

The Fool said to the disguised Kent, "Sirrah, you had best take my coxcomb."

"Sirrah" was a title used when addressing a person of inferior social status.

"Why, Fool?" the disguised Kent asked.

"Why, for taking the part of a person who is out of favor," the Fool said. "If you can't smile as the wind sits, you will catch cold shortly. If you can't curry favor with the people in power, you will find yourself out in the cold. So there, take my coxcomb. Why, this fellow has banished two of his daughters, and did the third a blessing against his will; if you follow him, you had better wear my coxcomb because you will be a fool."

King Lear had banished, in a way, his two older daughters. When he had possessions and power, they had shown respect to him. Now that they had his possessions and power, they no longer needed to show respect to him. King Lear had "banished" his two older daughters out of his intimate circle of family. He had also given Cordelia a blessing — although unintentionally

— by disinheriting her and not giving the dowry to her husband that he had promised to give. Because of this, Cordelia had not married the materialistic Duke of Burgundy; instead, she was now Queen of France.

The Fool said to King Lear, "My uncle, I wish that I had two coxcombs and two daughters!"

"Why, my boy?" King Lear asked.

"If I gave my two daughters all my other possessions, I would keep my two coxcombs for myself. There's my coxcomb; beg another one from your daughters."

The Fool was calling King Lear twice the fool the Fool was.

"Take heed, sirrah," King Lear said. "Remember the whip."

Fools made jokes and entertained Kings; they had much leeway in what they could say, but if they went too far, they could be whipped. Right now, the Fool was calling the King a fool. The Fool was speaking truth to power — or former power — and King Lear did not like what he was hearing.

The Fool said to him, "Truth is a dog that must go to kennel outside; he must be whipped out of doors. In contrast, Lady the flattering bitch is allowed to stand by the fire and stink."

"This pains me!" King Lear said. He was beginning to wonder whether what the Fool said was true.

"Sirrah, I'll teach you a speech," the Fool said.

"Go ahead."

The Fool said, "Listen to it carefully, my uncle."

He sang this song:

*"Have more than you show,*

*"Speak less than you know,*

*"Lend less than you owe,*

*"Ride more than you walk,*

*"Learn more than you hear,*

*"Don't stake all on a single throw.*

*"Leave your drink and your whore,*

*"And keep indoors,*

*"And you shall have more*

*"Than two tens to a score."*

The Fool gave wise advice in the beginning of the song, but the conclusion was nonsensical. The hearers expected the song to end up something like "And you shall have more / As your net worth becomes more." However, sometimes we can do the right things and yet suffer a bad result. We can also do things for good reasons and yet suffer a bad result.

As an octogenarian, King Lear wanted to pass his power and possessions on to his daughters because he sincerely believed that they sincerely loved him. Much could be said in support of his decision, but the consequences of it were turning out not to be what he expected and he was beginning to suspect that he had acted wrongly, both in giving away all his wealth and power and in treating Cordelia badly. In many cases, as when an elderly parent is beginning to show signs of senile dementia, the elderly parent ought to become the ward of his or her children, but King Lear, although he was an octogenarian, was vigorous enough to go hunting with his Knights.

"This song is nothing, Fool," King Lear said.

"Then it is like the breath of a lawyer who has not received a fee," the Fool said. "Lawyers will not do good work until they are paid, and you have paid me nothing for my song. Can you make any use of nothing, my uncle?"

"Why, no, boy," King Lear said. "Nothing can be made out of nothing."

The Fool said to the disguised Kent, "Please, tell him that nothing is the amount the rent of his land comes to. He will not believe a Fool."

King Lear had given away all his land — and all the income that his land had formerly brought him. Now he had no income; he had only the allowance his two older daughters were supposed to give him — an allowance that was supposed to include the pay of a hundred Knights to attend him.

"This is a bitter and sarcastic Fool!" King Lear said.

"Do you know the difference, my boy, between a bitter fool and a sweet fool?" the Fool asked.

"No, lad," King Lear replied. "Teach me."

"That lord who counseled you to give away all your land, place him here by me," the Fool said. "You can stand for him. The sweet fool and the bitter fool will immediately appear."

He pointed to himself and said, "The sweet one is the one in motley here."

He pointed to King Lear and said, "The bitter one is the one found there."

No lord had counseled King Lear to give away all his land; it had been the King's own idea.

"Do you call me fool, boy?" King Lear asked.

Speaking truth to former power, the Fool said, "All your other titles you have given away; the title of 'fool' is the one you were born with. You cannot give it away."

The disguised Kent, who was another man who had spoken truth to power, said to King Lear, "This is not altogether fool, my lord." He meant that what the Fool was saying was not altogether foolish, but instead included much sense.

The Fool deliberately misunderstood the sentence as saying that the Fool did not have all the foolishness of the world. He said, "No, truly, for the lords and great men will not let me have all the foolishness. Even if I had a monopoly on foolishness, they would have part of it. And this is true of ladies, too — they will not let me have all the foolishness to myself; they'll be snatching foolishness away from me."

The Fool paused, and then he added, "Give me an egg, my uncle, and I'll give you two crowns."

Crowns are coins, and they are the headwear of a King, and they are the tops of heads.

"What two crowns shall they be?" King Lear asked.

"Why, after I have cut the egg in the middle, and eaten up the egg, what will remain will be the two halves of the eggshell — the two crowns of the egg."

King Lear had given away his valuables: his land and his income. He had kept the title of King, but that was getting him little respect now.

The Fool continued, "When you split your crown in the middle, and gave away both parts, you behaved as foolishly as if you carried your donkey on your back as you trod over the dirt — you had as little wit in your bald crown when you gave your golden crown away. If I speak like myself — a Fool — in saying this, then let the person who first finds it true be whipped. Such a person is a Fool, and Fools are whipped, and such a person tells the truth, and people who tell the truth in this society are whipped."

The Fool sang this song:

*"Fools had never less wit in a year;*

*"For wise men are grown foolish,*

*"They know not how their wits to wear,*

"*Their manners are so apish.*"

The Fool's song stated that fools were not much needed now because wise men were acting like fools — the wise men were imitating, aka aping, fools.

King Lear asked, "Since when have you been so full of songs, sirrah?"

"I have made a habit of singing, my uncle, ever since you made your daughters your mothers, for when you gave them the whip, and pulled down your own pants —"

The Fool sang this song:

"*Then they for sudden joy did weep,*

"*And I for sorrow sung,*

"*That such a King should act like a child,*

"*And go among the fools.*"

The Fool added, "Please, my uncle, keep a schoolmaster who can teach your Fool to lie: I would like to learn to lie."

"If you lie, sirrah, we'll have you whipped," King Lear said, using the royal plural.

"I wonder how you and your daughters are related," the Fool said. "They'll have me whipped for speaking the truth, you will have me whipped for lying, and sometimes I am whipped for holding my peace and saying nothing. I had rather be any kind of thing than a Fool, and yet I would not be you, my uncle — you have pared your wit on both sides, and left nothing in the middle."

A Fool is supposed to be a half-wit, but King Lear had given away all of his wits along with everything else.

The Fool looked at the door and said, "Here comes one of the parings."

Frowning, Goneril entered the hall.

"How are you, daughter!" King Lear said. "Your frown looks like a frontlet — a band going across your forehead. I think that you have been frowning too much lately."

The Fool said to King Lear, "You were a fine fellow when you had no need to care about her frowning; now you are a zero without a number in front of it to give it value. I am better than you are now; I am a Fool, but you are nothing."

Angry, Goneril frowned at the Fool.

The Fool said to Goneril, "Yes, indeed, I will hold my tongue; so your face orders me to, although you say nothing. Mum, mum."

He sang this song:

*"He who keeps neither crust nor crumb,*

*"Tired of everything, shall want some."*

Crust and crumb referred specifically to a loaf of bread, but metaphorically to everything. The Fool was saying that King Lear had given away all he had, and that he would find himself wanting to have some of his wealth and power back.

The Fool pointed to King Lear and said, "That's a shelled peapod."

A shelled peapod is empty of peas, the valued part of the peapod; the shelled peapod itself is worth nothing.

Goneril said to King Lear, her father, "Not only, sir, this your all-licensed Fool, who is permitted to make fun of everyone and everything, but others of your insolent retinue hourly carp and quarrel, breaking forth in rank and gross and not-to-be-endured riots. Sir, I had thought, by making this well known to you, to have found a sure remedy; but now I grow fearful, because of what you yourself have spoken and done only recently, that you protect this kind of behavior and encourage it by being permissive. If this is true, you are committing a fault that will not escape censure. Remedies for this misbehavior must be found, although in order to get a wholesome and healthy society, these remedies might be thought to be an offence to you and cause me shame, except that the necessity for such remedies will silence such criticism and instead be praised as a sensible course of action."

The Fool said to King Lear, "For, you know, my uncle, the hedge-sparrow fed the cuckoo so long that it had its head bit off by its young. So, out went the candle, and we were left in the dark."

The cuckoo bird lays its eggs in the nests of other birds such as the hedge-sparrow, which rears the cuckoo's young, which grow larger than the hedge-sparrow and become a danger to it. The Fool's point in telling this story was that King Lear was in danger from his ungrateful daughter — who might not even be his biological daughter. At the very least, Goneril was not treating King Lear with the devotion that a biological daughter ought to feel for her father.

Shocked at this treatment from his daughter, King Lear asked, "Are you our daughter?"

He was pointing out that Goneril ought to treat him with the respect due a father.

"Come, sir," Goneril said, "I wish that you would make use of that good wisdom, of which I know that you have plenty, and put away these moods that recently have transformed you from what you rightly are."

The Fool said, "May not an ass know when the cart draws the horse?"

The Fool was pointing out that things were backwards here. The father can criticize a daughter, but the daughter ought not to criticize the father.

He sang, "*Whoop, Jug! I love you.*"

"Jug" was a nickname for "Joan," and "Joan" was a generic term for "whore."

King Lear asked sarcastically, "Does anyone here know me? This is not Lear. Does Lear walk like this? Does he speak like this? Where are his eyes? Either his mind weakens, or his faculties are paralyzed — am I awake? It is not so. Who is it who can tell me who I am?"

The Fool answered, "Lear's shadow — you are the shadow of King Lear."

"I would like to know who I am because by the signs of sovereignty, knowledge, and reason, I should be falsely persuaded I had daughters."

The Fool added, "— who will make you an obedient father."

King Lear asked Goneril sarcastically, "What is your name, fair gentlewoman?"

"This pretense of amazement, sir, is much of the savor of your other new pranks," Goneril said. "I ask you to understand my purposes correctly. As you are old and reverend, you should be wise. Here you are keeping a hundred Knights and squires; these men are so disordered, so debauched and bold, that our court, infected with their manners, looks like a riotous inn. Their pursuit of pleasure and lust makes our court more like a tavern or a brothel than a palace graced with the royal presence. This shame requires an immediate remedy; therefore, I ask that you — and if need be, I will forcefully take the thing I ask for — a little to reduce in number your train of followers. And let the remaining Knights, who shall still serve you, be such men as are suitable for your age, and know their own place and yours."

"Darkness and devils!" King Lear shouted. "Saddle my horses; call my train of followers together!"

He shouted at Goneril, "Degenerate bastard! I'll not trouble you any longer. I still have a daughter left."

Goneril said, "You physically strike my servants, and the members of your disordered rabble make servants of their betters."

The Duke of Albany, Goneril's husband, entered the hall.

King Lear said, "Woe to the person who repents too late."

He then said to the Duke of Albany, "Oh, sir, have you come? Is it your will? Speak, sir."

He ordered his followers, who were shocked and were still standing still, "Prepare my horses."

He then said to Goneril, "Ingratitude, you marble-hearted fiend, you are more hideous than a sea-monster when you show yourself in a child!"

"Please, sir, be patient," the Duke of Albany said to King Lear. "Control yourself."

King Lear said to Goneril, "Detested kite — you bird of prey! You lie! My train of followers are men of choice and rarest abilities who know all the particulars of their duty and exactly what they are to do, and they are very careful to live up to their excellent reputations."

He then said to himself, "Oh, very small fault, how ugly did you seem to be in Cordelia! That very small fault, like an engine, wrenched the frame of my nature from its fixed foundations like a building being pried up — it drew from my heart all love for Cordelia and added to my bitterness."

He hit himself in the head and shouted, "Oh Lear, Lear, Lear! Beat at this gate that let your folly and foolishness in and let your dear and considered judgment out!"

He said to his train of followers, "Let's go; go, my people."

The disguised Kent and the Knights left. The Fool remained.

The Duke of Albany said, "My lord, I am as guiltless as I am ignorant of what has upset you."

"That may be true, my lord," King Lear said.

He then cursed his daughter: "Hear, Nature, hear; dear goddess, hear! Suspend your purpose, if you intended to make this creature fruitful! Into her womb convey sterility! Dry up in her the organs of increase and birth and from her dishonored body never allow a babe to spring and honor her! If she must teem with an infant, create her child of spleen, so that it may live and be a perverse and unnatural torment to her! Let it stamp wrinkles in her youthful brow. Let it fret channels of falling tears in her cheeks. Let it turn all her mother's pains and beneficial care of her child to mocking laughter and contempt so that she may feel how sharper than a serpent's tooth it is to have a thankless and ungrateful child!"

He shouted, "Away! Away! Let's leave!"

He exited.

The Duke of Albany asked his wife, Goneril, "Now, by the gods whom we adore, what is the cause of this?"

She replied, "Never afflict yourself by knowing the cause; instead, let his disposition have the scope that dotage gives it."

King Lear returned; he was crying with anger.

He shouted, "What! Fifty of my followers released in a single moment! Within a fortnight of my giving you wealth and power!"

"What's the matter, sir?" the Duke of Albany asked.

King Lear replied, "I'll tell you."

He said to Goneril, "Life and death! I am ashamed that you have the power to shake my manhood like this. I am ashamed that you can cause these hot tears, which break from me involuntarily. I am ashamed that you are worth the tears of a King. May pestilential gusts and fogs of unhealthy air fall upon you! May the very deep wounds — too deep to be probed and cleansed — of a father's curse pierce every sense you have and cause you pain!"

He shouted, "Old foolish eyes, if you weep because of this cause again, I'll pluck you out, and cast you, with the tears that you shed, on the ground to mix with clay.

"Has it come to this? Let it be so. I still have a daughter left who, I am sure, is kind and will offer comfort to her father. When she shall hear this about you, she'll flay your wolvish visage with her fingernails. You shall find that I'll resume the Kingly appearance that you think I have cast off forever. You shall — that I promise you!"

King Lear exited again. The Fool remained again.

Goneril said to her husband, "Did you see that, my lord?"

Preparatory to criticizing her, he said, "I cannot be so partial, Goneril, to the great love I bear you —"

"Be quiet, please," Goneril said.

She called, "Oswald, come here!"

She said to the Fool, "You, sir, are more knave than Fool. Follow your master."

The Fool called, "My uncle Lear, my uncle Lear, tarry and take the Fool with you."

He sang this song:

"*A fox, when one has caught her,*

"*And such a daughter,*

"*Should surely be sent to the slaughter,*

"*If my Fool's cap would buy a halter, aka a noose,*

"*And so the Fool follows after his master.*"

The Fool exited.

Goneril said sarcastically, "This man has had 'good' counsel."

She meant that this man — her father — had NOT received good counsel from the Fool.

She added, "A hundred Knights!"

She said sarcastically, "It is 'politic' and 'safe' to let him keep armed and ready a hundred Knights. Yes, that way on every dream, each rumor, each fancy, each complaint, and each dislike, he may protect his dotage with their powers, and hold our lives at his mercy."

She shouted, "Oswald, I say!"

The Duke of Albany said, "Well, you may be fearing something that will not happen."

"That is safer than being too trustful," she replied. "Let me always take away the harms I fear; that is better than always fearing to be taken by harms. I know my father's heart. What he has uttered, I have ordered to be written to my sister. If she should sustain him and his hundred Knights after I have showed their unfitness —"

Oswald entered the hall.

"How is it going now, Oswald?" Goneril asked. "Have you written that letter to my sister?"

"Yes, madam."

"Take with you some company, and ride away on horseback and deliver the letter to my sister. Inform her in full of my particular fears, and add to them such reasons of your own as may strengthen it more. Go now, and quickly return."

Oswald exited.

Her husband was looking at her. He was not pleased.

Goneril said to him, "No, no, my lord, your mild and gentle way of acting — although I myself do not condemn it — yet, begging your pardon, other people much more criticize you for lacking wisdom than praise you for your harmful mildness. Your leniency can result in danger."

He replied, "How far your eyes may pierce the future I cannot tell; however, when we strive to make something better, often we mar what's already well."

Goneril started to speak: "No, because —"

He cut her off: "Well, we will see what the result of your actions will be."

In the courtyard of the Duke of Albany's palace stood King Lear, the disguised Kent, and the Fool.

King Lear said to the disguised Kent, "Go ahead of us to Gloucester with this letter. Acquaint my daughter no further with anything you know than comes from her questions about the letter. Do not volunteer information. Be diligent in your journey; otherwise, I shall be there before you."

"I will not sleep, my lord, until I have delivered your letter," the disguised Kent said.

He exited.

The Fool said, "If a man's brains were in his heels, wouldn't it be in danger of suffering from chilblains?"

A chilblain is a painful and itchy swelling on skin that has been exposed to cold and then rapidly warmed up.

King Lear replied, "Yes, boy."

"Then you ought to be merry because your wit and intelligence shall never go slipshod."

King Lear laughed at the joke. He would not have to wear slippers — be slipper-shod — because he would not have chilblains on his brains. And it was good news that his brains would not be slipshod — characterized by disorganization and a lack of thought.

But why wouldn't his brains be in his heels? One possible answer that was consistent with other things that the Fool had said was that King Lear had no brains. He had lost his brains — his wits — when he gave away his wealth and power.

The Fool said, "You shall see that your other daughter will treat you kindly because although she's as like this daughter — Goneril — as a crab is like an apple, yet I can tell what I can tell. I know what I know."

The Fool did not think that Regan would treat King Lear better than Goneril had treated him — he was punning. Regan would treat her father "kindly" — after her "kind." Unfortunately, her kind was not good.

The Fool also thought about King Lear's daughters Goneril and Regan that one daughter was as like the other daughter as a crab is to an apple. That may sound like the two daughters are very different, but the "crab" that the Fool was referring to was a crabapple.

"Why, what do you know, my boy?" King Lear asked.

"She will taste as like this daughter as a crab tastes like a crab."

In other words, the two daughters are exactly alike. Unfortunately, crabapples are small and sour.

The Fool then asked, "Do you know why one's nose stands in the middle of one's face?"

"No."

"Why, to keep one's eyes on either side of his nose so that what a man cannot smell out, he may spy into."

In other words, the Fool was advising King Lear to stay alert and learn something. He did not yet know the true nature of his daughter Regan.

Thinking about Cordelia, King Lear said, "I did her wrong —"

The Fool asked him, "Do you know how an oyster makes its shell?"

"No."

"Neither do I, but I know why a snail has a house."

"Why?"

"Why, to put his head in it; that way, he will not give it away to his daughters, and leave his horns without a case."

This was in part an indecent joke. Readers should already know what a man's "horn" is, and the word "case" in this society could refer to a vagina. The Fool could also have been referring to a cuckold's horns — a man with an unfaithful wife was depicted in pictures as having horns. Again, the Fool was hinting that Goneril and Regan were not legitimate — the assumption being that a legitimate daughter would love and respect and honor her father.

"I will forget my paternal nature," King Lear said. "Fathers are supposed to have a kindly nature when it comes to a daughter. I have been so kind a father! Are my horses ready?"

"Your asses have gone to get them ready," the Fool said.

He added, "The reason why the seven stars — the Pleiades — are no more than seven is a pretty fine reason."

"Because they are not eight?" King Lear said.

"Yes, indeed," the Fool said. "You would make a good Fool."

A good Fool should know what is obvious, even when it is not obvious to other people.

King Lear said to himself, thinking about Goneril, "Maybe I should take my Kingdom back by force! She has shown monstrous ingratitude to me!"

"If you were my Fool, my uncle, I would have you beaten because you are old before your time," the Fool said.

"How's that?"

"You should not have become old until you had become wise."

A gentleman walked over to them and King Lear asked him, "Are the horses ready?"

"They are ready, my lord."

"Come, boy," King Lear said to the Fool.

The Fool said, "She who's a virgin now, and laughs at my departure, shall not be a maiden long, unless things be cut shorter."

A young virgin who laughed at the Fool's departure was very foolish, in the Fool's opinion, because the Fool knew — based on his knowledge of Regan — that bad things were going to happen very soon. Such a virgin was too foolish to remain a virgin for very long unless men's things — the dangly longish sexual part under the front of their waist — should be cut very short.

# CHAPTER 2

## — 2.1 —

Edmund and the courtier Curan met in a room of the Earl of Gloucester's castle. They were close to where Edmund had hidden Edgar.

Edmund said, "May God save you, Curan."

"And you, sir. I have been with your father and have informed him that the Duke of Cornwall and Regan, his Duchess, will be here with him tonight."

"Why are they coming here?"

"I don't know. Have you heard of the news going around — I mean the whispered news, for it is so far only ear-kissing gossip?"

"No, I haven't heard it yet. What are people whispering?"

"Have you heard anything about a probable war between the Duke of Cornwall and the Duke of Albany?"

"Not a word," Edmund replied.

"You may hear something, then, soon. Fare you well, sir."

Curan exited.

Edmund said to himself, "The Duke of Cornwall is coming here tonight? This is better than I could imagine! This is the best thing that could possibly happen! His coming here weaves itself necessarily into my plot — I can take advantage of this! My father is ready to accuse and arrest my brother, and I have one thing, of a queasy question, aka sensitive nature, that I must do. May speed and good fortune be on my side and help me!"

He called, "Brother, may I have a word with you? Descend, brother, I say!"

Edgar entered the room.

"My father is still awake and watchful. Oh, sir, flee from this place; my father has been given information about where you are hiding. You have now the good advantage of the night so you can escape unseen. Haven't you spoken against the Duke of Cornwall? He's coming here, now, in the night, hastily, and Regan is with him. Have you said nothing about supporting his side against the Duke of Albany? Think."

"I am sure that I have not said a word," Edgar replied.

"I hear my father coming," Edmund said. "Pardon me. As part of a deception, I must draw my sword upon you. Draw your sword; seem to defend yourself; now act as if you were fighting me fiercely."

Edmund said loudly so that his father would hear, "Surrender! Appear before my father. Light! Bring light here!"

He said softly, "Flee from here, brother."

Then he shouted, "Torches! Bring torches!"

He said softly to Edgar, "And so, farewell."

Edgar exited.

Edmund said softly to himself, "Some blood drawn from me would help create the opinion that Edgar and I have really been fiercely fighting."

He used his sword to lightly wound and bloody his arm.

He said softly, "I have seen drunkards do more than this in sport."

Young men of the time would sometimes wound themselves so that they could drink a toast of blood and wine to their beloved.

He shouted, "Father! Father! Stop! Stop! Won't anyone help me?"

The Earl of Gloucester entered the room, along with some servants who were carrying torches.

"Now, Edmund, where's the villain?" the Earl of Gloucester asked.

Edmund, who wanted Edgar to get away lest their father's questions reveal the truth about what had happened, delayed answering the question. He said, "Here he stood in the dark, his sharp sword out, mumbling wicked charms, conjuring the Moon to be his auspicious mistress and help him —"

"But where is he?" the Earl of Gloucester asked.

Still playing for time, Edmund said, "Look, sir, I am bleeding."

"Where is the villain, Edmund?"

Pointing in the wrong direction, Edmund replied, "He fled this way, sir. When by no means he could —"

The Earl of Gloucester ordered, "Pursue him! Go after him!"

Some servants exited in pursuit of Edgar.

He asked Edmund, "By no means what?"

"Persuade me to murder your lordship," Edmund replied. "I told him that the avenging gods aim all their lightning and thunder against parricides — people who murder their own father. I spoke about the manifold and strong bonds that bind the child to the father. Sir, at last Edgar, seeing how I loathed and opposed his unnatural purpose, in one deadly motion thrust his drawn and ready sword at me and attacked my unprotected body and cut my arm. But when he saw my courage aroused as if in response to a battle cry — I was brave because I knew that I was in the right — and saw that I was ready to fight back, or perhaps because he was frightened by the noise I made, quite suddenly he fled."

"Let him fly far," the Earl of Gloucester said. "If he stays in this land, he shall be caught, and when he is found, he will be killed. The noble Duke of Cornwall, who is my master, my worthy and honorable overlord and patron, comes here tonight. By his authority I will proclaim that whoever finds Edgar shall deserve our thanks for bringing the murderous coward to the place of execution; the penalty for whoever conceals Edgar shall be death."

Edmund said, "When I tried to convince him not to try to have you killed and found him completely determined to do it, with angry speech I threatened to reveal his plot. He replied, 'You beggarly bastard who is legally prevented from inheriting his property, do you think, if I would oppose you, that any trust, virtue, or worth in you would make your words believed? No! I would deny everything even if you were to produce evidence in the form of a letter written in my own handwriting — I would say that everything was your suggestion, plot, and damned practice. You must think that everyone in the world is a dullard if they would not realize that you, Edmund, would greatly profit if I, Edgar, were to die: You would inherit our father's property. That is an understandable and powerful motive for you to seek my death!'"

"He is an unnatural and hardened villain!" the Earl of Gloucester said. "Would he deny having written his letter? I never fathered him — he is no son of mine!"

Some trumpets sounded the distinctive notes that announced the arrival of the Duke of Cornwall.

The Earl of Gloucester said, "Listen, the Duke's trumpets! I don't know why he is coming here."

He then said, "I'll close all the seaports; the villain Edgar shall not escape; the Duke of Cornwall must grant me that privilege. In addition, I will send Edgar's picture far and near, so that everyone in the Kingdom may have the information they need about him.

"And, Edmund, you loyal and loving boy, I'll work the legal means that will make you capable of inheriting my land."

The Duke of Cornwall, Regan, and some attendants entered the room.

The Duke of Cornwall said, "How are you now, my noble friend! Ever since I came here, which was just now, I have heard strange news."

"If it is true," Regan said, "all punishments are inadequate for the offender. How are you, my lord?"

"Oh, madam, my old heart is cracked! It's cracked!" the Earl of Gloucester cried.

"What! Did my father's godson really seek your life? He whom my father named? Your Edgar?"

"Oh, lady, lady, my shame would like this to be hidden and not known!"

"Wasn't he the companion of the riotous Knights who serve my father?" Regan asked.

"I don't know, madam," the Earl of Gloucester said. "This situation is very bad — very bad!"

Taking advantage of an opportunity to further slime Edgar, Edmund said, "Yes, madam, he was one of that group."

Regan replied, "It is no wonder this happened, then, even if Edgar were disloyal. It is those riotous Knights who have invited him to kill the old man — his father — so that they can spend and waste his income. I have this evening received a letter from my sister, Goneril, who has well informed me about these riotous Knights. She gave such warnings that I decided that if they come to stay at my house, I will not be there."

"Nor I, I assure you, Regan," the Duke of Cornwall said.

He added, "Edmund, I hear that you have shown your father the loyalty that a child owes a father."

"It was my duty, sir," Edmund replied.

"Edmund revealed Edgar's plot, and he received this injury you see on his arm while striving to apprehend him," the Earl of Gloucester said.

"Is Edgar being pursued?" the Duke of Cornwall asked.

"Yes, my good lord," the Earl of Gloucester replied.

"If he is captured, you shall never again fear that he will do harm — he will be killed," the Duke of Cornwall said. "Use my resources to do what you think needs to be done."

Using the royal plural, he added, "As for you, Edmund, whose virtue and obedience that you have shown just now do so much to commend you, you shall serve us. Natures of such deep trust and loyalty we shall much need. We choose you to enter our service."

"I shall serve you, sir, truly and loyally, above all else," Edmund replied.

"For him I thank your Grace," the Earl of Gloucester said.

The Duke of Cornwall began to say, "You don't know why we came to visit you —"

Regan interrupted, "— thus out of season, threading dark-eyed night as we avoided obstacles as we traveled through the darkness. Matters, noble Gloucester, of some importance have arisen about which we must have your advice. Our father has written to us, and so has our sister, about quarrels between them. I thought it fitting and best to answer our father's letter while we are away from our home. Several messengers are waiting to be sent back with our reply. Our good old friend, console yourself about Edgar's disloyalty to you, and give us the advice we need about this matter, which needs to be taken care of immediately."

The Earl of Gloucester replied, "I will help you, madam. Your graces are very welcome."

The disguised Kent and the undisguised Oswald, Goneril's steward, met in front of the Earl of Gloucester's castle. The time was a little before dawn.

Oswald said, "Good dawning to you, friend. Are you a servant in this castle?"

The disguised Kent replied, "Yes."

This was a lie. He recognized Oswald, whom he had tripped in the Duke of Albany's castle because Oswald had treated King Lear badly, and he wanted to start a fight with him. Oswald did not recognize Kent.

"Where may we stable our horses?" Oswald asked.

"In the mud and mire," the disguised Kent replied.

"Please, if you respect me, tell me."

"If you respect me" meant "if you would be so kind," but the disguised Kent deliberately mistook it as being literal.

"I don't respect you."

"Why, then, I don't care for you," an angry Oswald replied.

"If I had you in Lipsbury pinfold, I would make you care for me."

A pinfold is a pen for stray cattle, and "Lipsbury" has the meaning of "Lipstown." The disguised Kent was saying that if he had Oswald in his power — between his teeth — he would make him care for — be wary of — him.

"Why are you talking to and treating me this way?" Oswald complained. "I don't know you."

"Fellow, I know you," the disguised Kent said.

"Who do you think I am?"

"You are a knave. You are a rascal. You are a servant who dines on broken foods — leftovers. You are a base, proud, shallow, beggarly, three-suited, lightweight, filthy, worsted-stocking knave. You have only the three suits of clothing given annually to servants, and you wear the low-value worsted stockings that a servant wears rather than the silk stockings of an upper-class person. You are a lily-livered, legal-action-taking knave who is too cowardly to fight and so prefers to file a lawsuit. You are a whoreson, mirror-gazing and vain, super-serviceable and over-officious as well as finical and fussy rogue. You are a one-trunk-inheriting slave — all you inherited will fit into one trunk. You are a person who will be a bawd by way of providing good service to your master. You are nothing but the compound of a knave, beggar, coward, and panderer. You are the son and heir of a mongrel bitch; not only are you a son of a mongrel bitch, but you also inherited all the qualities of the mongrel bitch. You are a person whom I will beat into clamorous whining if you deny even the smallest syllable of the names that I have called you."

Oswald complained, "Why, what a monstrous fellow you are, thus to rail against a person whom you do not know and who does not know you!"

"What a brazen-faced varlet you are to deny that you know me!" the disguised Kent said. "Is it two days since I tripped up your heels, and beat you in front of the King? Draw your sword, you rogue, for although it is night, yet the Moon shines. I'll make a sop of the moonlight out of you: I will fill you full of holes that soak up the moonlight. Draw your sword, you whoreson, despicable barber-monger, draw."

Kent was a master of invective. A whoremonger is a person who drums up business for whores. Kent was calling Oswald a barber-monger, a person who drummed up business for barbers. In other words, he was saying that Oswald made himself useful to men who were very concerned about their appearance.

Kent drew his sword.

Oswald said, "Stay away from me! I have nothing to do with you."

"Draw, you rascal. You have come with letters against the King, and you take the part of Vanity the Puppet — Goneril — against the royalty of her father. Draw, you rogue, or I'll slice your shanks. Draw your sword, you rascal, and fight me!"

Oswald shouted, "Help! Murder! Help!"

"Fight, you slave! Stand up and fight, rogue! Stand! You fancy slave, fight!"

The disguised Kent used the flat of his sword to hit Oswald.

Oswald shouted again, "Help! Murder! Help!"

Edmund, who had drawn his rapier, arrived on the scene, as did Regan, the Earl of Gloucester, and some servants.

Edmund asked, "What's the matter?"

The disguised Kent replied, "Let us fight, impudent boy, if you please. Come, I'll wound your flesh and initiate you into the world of adults. Come on, young master."

The Earl of Gloucester said, "Weapons! Arms! What's the matter here?"

The Duke of Cornwall ordered, "Stop fighting. Keep the peace. Your lives depend upon it. Whoever strikes again with his weapon will die. What is the matter?"

Regan said, "These are the messengers from our sister and from the King."

"What is your argument about?" the Duke of Cornwall asked. "Speak!"

"I am out of breath, my lord," Oswald replied.

"That is not a surprise since you have 'fought' so 'courageously,'" the disguised Kent said sarcastically to him. "You cowardly rascal, Nature refuses to admit that you are natural. In fact, a tailor made you."

"You are a strange fellow," the Duke of Cornwall said. "Can a tailor make a man?"

"Yes, a tailor did, sir," the disguised Kent said. "A stone-cutter or painter could not have made him so badly, even if he had been only two hours at the job. The man the tailor made is not a man; he is a tailor's dummy."

"Speak," the Duke of Cornwall ordered Oswald. "How did your quarrel begin?"

"This ancient ruffian, sir, whose life I have spared because of his gray beard —"

Insulted, the disguised Kent said. "You whoreson zed! You unnecessary letter!"

The letter Z did not appear in dictionaries of the time. People felt that the letter Z was unnecessary because it could be replaced by the letter S and because Latin did not have a letter Z.

The disguised Kent said to the Duke of Cornwall, "My lord, if you will give me leave, I will tread this unbolted villain into mortar, and daub the wall of a privy with him. Spare my gray beard, you wagtail?"

The disguised Kent's insults continued. "Unbolted" had the meaning of "unsifted"; Kent would have to step continually on Oswald in order to get the lumps out of the mortar. Of course, if Oswald were unbolted, he was not locked up in a jail. Also, if Oswald were "unbolted," he lacked a man's "bolt." In addition, a wagtail is a bird that bobs its tail up and down. Kent was suggesting that Oswald was an obsequious courtier who was constantly bowing. He may also have meant that Oswald was excitedly hopping and unable to keep still.

The Duke of Cornwall ordered, "Shut up, sirrah! You beastly knave, know you no reverence and respect?"

"Yes, sir, I do, but anger has a privilege," the disguised Kent said.

"Why are you angry?" the Duke of Cornwall asked.

"I am angry that such a slave as this should wear a sword, which is a privilege given to gentlemen, not to a man such as this who has no honesty and no virtue. Such smiling rogues as this Oswald, like rats, often bite the holy cords of marriage in two that are too intricately and closely knotted to be untied."

The disguised Kent was making a major insinuation that Oswald was helping his boss, Goneril, sin against her husband, the Duke of Cornwall. Previously, he had called Oswald a panderer — a go-between between two illicit lovers.

He added, "Such smiling rogues smooth the path of their lords' passions that rebel against reason — they help their lords satisfy their unreasonable desires. They bring oil to fire, and they bring snow to their masters' colder moods.

"They deny, affirm, and turn their halcyon beaks with every varying gale of their masters. They say no when their masters want to hear no, and they say yes when their masters want to hear yes. They are like a dead kingfisher that has been hung up by its neck; whichever way the wind blows the dead kingfisher will turn so that its beak acts like a weathervane.

"They know nothing, like dogs, except how to follow their masters."

Seeing Oswald looking with contempt at him, the disguised Kent shouted at him, "A plague upon your epileptic visage! Are you smiling at what I have to say, as if I were a fool? Goose, if I had you upon Salisbury plain, I would drive you cackling home to Camelot."

"What? Are you insane, old fellow?" the Duke of Cornwall asked.

"How did you two fall out?" the Earl of Gloucester asked. "Why did you two grow angry at each other? Tell us that."

"No two opposites hate each other more than I and this knave," the disguised Kent said.

"Why do you call him a knave? What's his offense?" the Duke of Cornwall asked.

"His face does not please me."

"And, perhaps, neither does mine, nor the Earl of Gloucester's, nor my Duchess.'"

"Sir, it is my particular pastime to be plain," the disguised Kent said. "I have seen better faces in my time than stand on any shoulders that I see before me at this instant."

The Duke of Cornwall said, "This is some fellow who, having been praised for bluntness, puts on a saucy roughness, and forces plain-speaking away from its true nature. He uses it not for honest candor but for crafty trickery. This man cannot flatter — not he! He has an honest and plain mind — he must speak the truth! If they will endure his talk, he has won a victory over them; if they will not, he says that he is plain-spoken. These kinds of knaves I know; in this plain-spokenness they hide more craft and trickery and corrupter ends than twenty silly ducking attendants who constantly make silly and obsequious bows."

The disguised Kent mocked the Duke of Cornwall by using elevated, not plain, language: "Sir, in good sooth, in sincere verity, under the allowance of your great aspect, whose influence, like the wreath of radiant fire on flickering Phoebus Apollo's forehead —"

The Duke of Cornwall asked, "What do you mean by this?"

"I mean to go out of my usual style of speaking, which you criticize so much. I know, sir, that I am no flatterer: Whoever he was who deceived you with plain talk was a plain knave, which for my part I will not be, even though I may be so plain-spoken that you think that I am a plain knave."

The Duke of Cornwall said to Oswald, "What was the offense you committed against him?"

"I never did him any offense," Oswald replied. "It pleased the King his master very recently to strike at me because he misunderstood something. At that time, this man, in league with and wanting to encourage the King in his displeasure, tripped me from behind. Once I was down on the floor, he insulted me and railed against me. He acted in such a macho manner that the King thought that he was a hero and praised him although all he had done was to attack someone who was willing to walk away from a fight. Because of his success in attacking a man who would not fight back, he drew his sword against me here and attacked me again."

The disguised Kent said, "None of these rogues and cowards but Ajax is their Fool."

This meant: *Rogues and cowards surround me, and Ajax is their Fool.* Not surprisingly, this was another major insult. Great Ajax was a warrior hero in Homer's *Iliad,* but later his reputation declined and he gained a reputation for great stupidity. Kent was saying that among these rogues and cowards, Ajax would be the Fool. As shown by King Lear's Fool, Fools are not foolish although fools are foolish. In fact, Fools are often wise. Kent was saying that Ajax, as foolish as he was, would be the wise man in this group of people around him.

Instantly angry, the Duke of Cornwall ordered, "Bring the stocks here!"

He wanted to punish the disguised Kent by putting him in the stocks, which would restrain his legs so that he could not move. The stocks were used to punish lower-class people who had committed misdemeanors.

The Duke of Cornwall said to the disguised Kent, "You stubborn old knave, you reverend braggart, we'll teach you —"

The disguised Kent, as plain-spoken as ever, interrupted, "Sir, I am too old to learn. Call not your stocks for me. I serve the King, on whose employment I was sent to you. You shall do small respect and show too bold malice against the grace and person of my master if you stock his messenger."

The disguised Kent was correct. Because he served King Lear, he ought to be respected because of the King. If the Duke of Cornwall were to put him in the stocks, he would be gravely insulting Lear both as a King and as a man.

The Duke of Cornwall ordered, "Bring the stocks here! As I have life and honor, there shall he sit until noon."

Regan said, "Until noon? Until night, my lord — and all night, too!"

"Why, madam, even if I were your father's dog, you should not treat me so."

"Sir, you are my father's knave, and so I will treat you so."

The Duke of Cornwall said, "This is a fellow who matches the description of the people our sister-in-law Goneril warned us against. Come, bring the stocks!"

The stocks were brought out.

The Earl of Gloucester said, "Let me beg your grace not to do this. His fault is great, and the good King his master will rebuke him for it. Your purposed low correction — the stocks — is such as is used to punish the basest and most contemptible wretches for such things as small thefts and other common crimes. The King must take it ill that he's so slightly valued that his messenger is thus restrained."

"I'll answer that," the Duke of Cornwall said. "I'll take responsibility for this."

Regan said, "My sister may take it much more worse to have her gentleman — Oswald — abused and assaulted for following her orders. Put his legs in the stocks."

The disguised Kent was put in the stocks.

Regan said, "Come, my good lord, let's leave."

Everyone left except the Earl of Gloucester and the disguised Earl of Kent, who was undergoing a humiliating punishment that ought never to be inflicted on an Earl.

"I am sorry for you, friend," the Earl of Gloucester said. "This is the Duke's pleasure, whose disposition, all the world well knows, will not be hindered or stopped. I'll entreat him to release you."

"Please do not, sir," the disguised Kent said. "I have been awake a long time and travelled hard; some of the time I spend in the stocks I shall sleep, and the rest of the time I'll whistle. A good man's fortune may poke out at heels."

A good man's fortune may wear away until it becomes bad fortune, just like a good stocking becomes a bad stocking when it wears out and one's heel pokes out of it.

The disguised Kent then said, "May God give you a good morrow!"

"The Duke's to blame in this; it will be ill taken," the Earl of Gloucester said, and then he exited.

Kent said to himself, "Good King Lear, you must prove this common proverb to be true: You out of Heaven's benediction come to the warm Sun, aka a place of no shelter! Yes, you must go from better to worse, from a place like Heaven to a place that is this Earth. You have been King, but here you will not be treated like a King. When you arrive here, bad things will happen."

He took out a letter and said softly, "Approach, you beacon — the Sun — to this under globe — the Earth — so that by your comfortable beams I may read this letter! Nothing almost sees miracles but misery; in other words, no one but the truly miserable almost sees miracles. When one is truly miserable, one hopes for a miracle!

"I know this letter is from Cordelia, who has most fortunately been informed of my obscured course of action — of what I am doing while I am in disguise.

"Cordelia is in France, away from this enormous and broken state of affairs, and she is finding time to seek a way to give losses their remedies. She wishes to right all these wrongs.

"My eyes are completely weary from being awake too long, so take advantage, heavy eyes, of this opportunity to sleep and not look at these stocks — this shameful lodging.

"Fortune, good night. Smile once more on me, and turn your wheel! Right now, I am at the bottom of the Wheel of Fortune, and a turn of the wheel will bring me higher."

He slept.

Edgar thought out loud in a wooded area: "I heard myself proclaimed to be an outlaw, and I was lucky and happy to find and hide in a hollow of a tree and so escape the hunt.

"No seaport is free and open to me; everyplace has guards who watch with very unusual vigilance and hope to capture me. As long as I can escape capture, I will preserve myself. I have formed the plan to take the basest and poorest shape that ever poverty, in contempt of man, has brought a man closest to being a beast.

"I'll grime my face with filth, cover only my loins and leave the rest naked, neglect my hair until it is matted and knotted, and exposed and naked I will confront the winds and persecutions of the sky.

"The countryside gives me examples and precedents of Bedlam beggars — former inmates of the Bethlehem Hospital for the insane who, released and with a license to beg, with roaring voices, stick in their numbed and pain-insensitive bare arms pins, wooden skewers, nails, and sprigs of rosemary, and with this horrible spectacle, they force people from humble farms, poor and paltry villages, sheep-cotes, and mills, sometimes with the use of lunatic curses, sometimes with prayers, to give them charity."

Edgar practiced the cries of a Bedlam beggar: "Poor Turlygod! Poor Tom!"

He then said, "There is some good in this for me. I will look nothing like Edgar."

King Lear, the Fool, and a gentleman who served King Lear arrived at the courtyard of the Earl of Gloucester's castle. They were close to the disguised Kent, King Lear's messenger, who was still in the stocks.

King Lear said, "It is strange that the Duke of Cornwall and Regan should depart in this way from their home, and not send back to me my messenger."

The gentleman said, "I learned that the night before they moved they had no plan to move."

They had not seen the disguised Kent, but now he said, "Hail to you, noble master!"

Seeing that the disguised Kent was in stocks, King Lear asked him, "Are you doing this for your own amusement? Is this a joke?"

"No, my lord."

The Fool said, "He is wearing cruel garters."

The Fool was punning on "crewel," which was a thin worsted yarn that was used to make stockings.

The Fool continued, "Horses are tied by the heads, dogs and bears by the neck, monkeys by the waist, and men by the legs. When a man's over-lusty at legs — a vagabond — then he wears wooden stockings."

King Lear asked the disguised Kent, "Who is the man who has so misunderstood your position as my messenger that he has placed you here in the stocks?"

"It is both he and she: your son-in-law and daughter."

Horrified, King Lear said, "No!" To deliberately stock his messenger — knowing that he was his messenger — was a major insult to him as a King and as a man and as a father and father-in-law.

"Yes."

"No, I say."

"I say, yes."

"No, no, they would not."

"Yes, they have."

"By Jupiter, I swear, no."

"By Juno, I swear, yes."

King Lear said, "They would not dare to do it. They could not, would not do it; it is worse than murder to do such violent outrage to a person whom they ought to respect because of whom he serves. Tell me, as quickly as you can tell me clearly, in which way you might deserve, or they might legitimately impose, this treatment on you, knowing that you are my messenger."

"My lord, when at their home I delivered your Highness' letter to them, before I rose from the place I was kneeling to show them respect, there came a steaming messenger, soaked in sweat because of his haste, half breathless, panting forth the salutations that came from Goneril. He delivered a letter, although he was interrupting me, which they read immediately. Because of the contents of that letter, the Duke of Cornwall and Regan summoned up their retinue of servants, immediately took to horse, and then commanded me to follow them and wait until they had leisure to answer your letter. They gave me cold looks.

"Meeting here in this place the other messenger, whose welcome, I perceived, had poisoned mine — he was Oswald, the very fellow who had recently been so saucy to your Highness — and having more courage than intelligence about me, I drew my sword.

"He aroused the people in the house with his loud and cowardly cries. Your son and daughter found this trespass worth the shame that here it suffers in the stocks."

The Fool said, "Winter's not gone yet, if the wild geese fly that way."

He meant that bad times were going to continue. If the wild geese were still flying south, winter was coming. Regan was acting the way that Goneril had acted.

The Fool then sang this song:

*"Fathers who wear rags*

*"Do make their children blind;*

*"But fathers who bear moneybags*

*"Shall see their children kind.*

*"Fortune, that arrant whore,*

*"Never turns the key to the poor."*

When a father is poor, his children will be blind to his needs because providing for his needs will cost them money. But when a father is rich, his children will be kind to him in hopes of receiving a good inheritance. Fortune, aka luck, is a whore who will not open her door to a poor man who cannot afford to pay her for her services.

The Fool added, "But, for all this, you shall have as many dolors — by which I mean griefs, not dollars — on account of your daughters as you can speak of or count in a year."

Feeling ill, King Lear said, "Oh, how this mother swells up toward my heart! *Hysterica passio*, go back down, you climbing sorrow. Your element's below!"

The illness *hysterica passio* was also called "the mother." The affliction involved a sense of choking and suffocation that began low and then went higher in the throat. It was thought to begin in the womb for women and in the abdomen for men.

King Lear asked, "Where is my daughter?"

The disguised Kent replied, "With the Earl of Gloucester, sir. She is within."

King Lear said to the gentleman and the Fool, "Don't follow me. Stay here."

He exited.

The gentleman asked the disguised Kent, "Did you commit any offense other than the one you spoke of?"

"None," Kent replied. "How is it that the King comes with so small a train of followers?"

The Fool said, "If you had been set in the stocks for asking that question, you would have well deserved it."

"Why, Fool?"

The Fool gave a cynical answer: "We'll send you to be educated by an ant, to teach you there's no laboring in the winter."

The Fool was saying that men do not work when they receive no profit. Ants work hard in the summer because food can be collected then, but they do not work in the winter. Similarly, many people were willing to serve King Lear when he had wealth and power, but many people were not willing to serve him now.

The Fool continued, "All who follow their noses are led by their eyes except blind men; and there's not a nose among twenty but can smell a man who is stinking."

The Fool was saying that it was obvious that King Lear lacked wealth and power. A sighted man could readily see his poverty, and a blind man could readily smell his poverty, which stank.

The Fool continued, "Let go your hold when a great wheel runs down a hill, lest it break your neck as you follow it, but when a great wheel goes up the hill, let it draw you upward."

In other words, hitch your wagon to a rising star, but when a star falls abandon it. Watch how your master's Wheel of Fortune is turning: Is it bringing him higher or lower?

The advice was cynical, but the Fool did not think that good people would, or should, follow it.

The Fool continued, "When a wise man gives you better advice than I have just given you, give my advice back to me. I want no one but knaves to follow this advice, since a fool gives it."

The Fool sang this song:

*"That sir who serves and seeks for gain,*

*"And follows but for form,*

*"Will pack when it begins to rain,*

*"And leave you in the storm."*

The word "form" meant "appearance." The Fool was saying that many men abandon the person they serve when the going gets rough.

He continued to sing this song:

*"But I will tarry; the Fool will stay,*

*"And let the wise man fly:*

*"The knave turns fool who runs away;*

*"The Fool is no knave, by God."*

The Fool was saying that he would continue to serve King Lear. Abandoning him would be a knavish thing to do, the kind of thing a fool would do, and the Fool was no knave and no fool.

The disguised Kent asked the Fool, "Where did you learn this, Fool?"

The Fool replied, "Not in the stocks, Fool."

This was a compliment. The Fool was saying that the disguised Kent was a faithful follower of King Lear and that the disguised Kent would not abandon him — the disguised Kent was no knave. If the disguised Kent had abandoned King Lear, he would not now be in the stocks.

King Lear returned with the Earl of Gloucester.

King Lear said, "They refuse to speak with me? They are sick? They are weary? They have travelled all night? These are mere excuses, tricks, and pretenses. These are signs of revolt and desertions. Go back to them and bring me a better answer."

The Earl of Gloucester replied, "My dear lord, you know the fiery quality of Duke Cornwall and how stubborn and fixed he is in his own course. He wants to have things his own way."

Angry, King Lear shouted, "Vengeance! Plague! Death! Destruction!"

He then shouted, "Fiery? What quality? Why, Gloucester, Gloucester, I wish to speak with the Duke of Cornwall and his wife."

"Well, my good lord, I have informed them so."

"Informed them!" King Lear said. "Do you understand me, man?"

"Yes, my good lord."

"The King wishes to speak with the Duke of Cornwall; the dear father wishes to speak with his daughter, and he commands her service and is waiting for her. Have they been informed of this? My breath and blood! Fiery? The fiery Duke? Tell the hot Duke that — no, do not tell him yet. Maybe he is not well. Illness always makes us neglect our duties that we would do if we were well and healthy. We are not ourselves when we are afflicted by illness that commands the mind to suffer with the body. I'll restrain myself, and I am angry that my headstrong impulse makes me mistake an indisposed and sickly man for a sound and healthy man."

His eyes happened to fall on the disguised Kent, who was still in the stocks, and he immediately grew angry again: "Death on my state! Why should he sit here? This act persuades me that this move of the Duke of Cornwall and Regan from their palace to here and their refusal to speak to me is a deliberate scheme and insult. Set my servant free. Go tell the Duke and his wife that I will speak with them now — immediately. Tell them to come here and listen to me, or at their chamber-door I'll beat a drum and kill their sleep."

"I would have all well between you," the Earl of Gloucester said as he left to carry out the errand.

Suffering another attack of *hysterica passio*, King Lear said, "Oh, me! My heart, my rising heart! Down!"

The Fool said, "Cry, my uncle, as the cockney cook did to the eels when she put them alive in the cooking dish; she rapped them on the heads with a stick, and cried, 'Down, playful creatures, down!'"

If the cockney cook had killed the eels before putting them in the cooking dish, she would not have had this problem.

If King Lear's heart had stopped and he had died before his wealth and power were distributed, he would not now be having this problem. And if Goneril and Regan had died earlier, King Lear would not now be having this problem.

The Fool added, "It was her brother who, in pure kindness to his horse, buttered its hay."

Her brother had wanted to be kind, but horses do not eat grease. The brother's kindness had a bad result: It rendered the hay inedible.

King Lear had wanted to be kind when he gave away his wealth and power as dowries for his daughters, but his kindness was having bad results.

The Duke of Cornwall, Regan, the Earl of Gloucester, and some servants arrived.

"Good morrow to you both," King Lear said to the Duke of Cornwall and Regan.

"Hail to your grace!" the Duke of Cornwall replied.

The servants set the disguised Kent free.

Regan said to her father, "I am glad to see your Highness."

"Regan, I think you are," King Lear said. "I know what reason I have to think so. If you should not be glad to see me, I would divorce your mother, who is in a tomb, because the tomb would be sepulchering an adulteress."

A biological daughter ought to be glad to see her father.

King Lear looked at the disguised Kent and said to him, "Oh, are you free? Some other time we will address that."

He then said, "Beloved Regan, your sister's evil. Oh, Regan, her sharp-toothed unkindness has stabbed me, like a vulture tied to me, here."

Overcome with emotion, he pointed to his heart, and then he said, "I can scarcely speak; you will not believe with how depraved a manner — oh, Regan!"

"Please, control yourself," Regan said. "I hope that you are mistaken. I hope that you are undervaluing Goneril's good qualities rather than that she is failing in her duties as a daughter to you."

"What do you mean?"

Regan replied, "I cannot think my sister in the least would fail in her obligations to you. If, sir, perhaps she has restrained the riotous behavior of your followers, it is on such grounds, and for such a wholesome end, as would clear her of all blame."

King Lear shouted, "My curses on her!"

Regan replied, "Oh, sir, you are old. Nature in you stands on the very verge of her limit — you have nearly reached the end of your life. You should be ruled and led by some discreet person who discerns your state of mind — and your social position — better than you yourself do. Therefore, I ask you to please return to our sister and say that you have wronged her, sir."

"Ask her for her forgiveness?" King Lear said. "Do you think that this would suit my position as King and father?"

He knelt and said, "Dear daughter, I confess that I am old. Old people are useless. On my knees I beg that you'll give me clothing, bed and shelter, and food."

Regan said, "Good sir, no more of this. This is an unsightly trick. Return to my sister."

King Lear stood up and said, "Never, Regan. She has deprived me of half of my train of followers. She has looked black upon me, and she struck me with her tongue, very like a serpent, upon the very heart. May all the stored vengeances of Heaven fall on her ungrateful head! Strike her young bones, you infecting airs, with lameness!"

"Sir!" the Duke of Cornwall said.

King Lear shouted, "You nimble lightnings, dart your blinding flames into her scornful eyes! Infect her beauty, you swampland fogs, drawn by the powerful Sun; fall upon her and blast her pride!"

Regan said, "Oh, the blest gods! You will wish the same things on me when you are in another rash mood."

"No, Regan, you shall never have my curse," King Lear said. "Your tender-hearted nature that is set in a woman's body shall not give you over to harshness. Goneril's eyes are fierce; but your eyes comfort and do not burn. It is not in you to begrudge me my pleasures, to reduce in size my train of followers, to exchange hasty words with me, to scant my allowance, and in conclusion to draw the bolt and lock the door to prevent me from coming in. You know better than Goneril the duties of natural affection, the bond of childhood, the good manners of courtesy, and the dues of gratitude — you have not forgotten the half of the Kingdom that I gave you."

"Good sir, get to the point," Regan said.

"Who put my servant in the stocks?" King Lear asked.

A trumpet sounded some distinctive notes.

"What trumpet is that?" the Duke of Cornwall asked.

"I know it," Regan said. "It is my sister's. In her letter to me, she wrote that she would come here."

Oswald, Goneril's courtier, entered the courtyard.

"Has your lady come?" Regan asked.

King Lear said about Oswald, "This is a slave, whose easy-borrowed pride dwells in the fickle grace of the woman he serves. He has done nothing to deserve pride; he has no rightful pride."

He said to Oswald, "Out, varlet; get out of my sight!"

Oswald stayed in the courtyard.

"What does your grace mean?" the Duke of Cornwall asked.

"Who put my servant in the stocks?" King Lear asked. "Regan, I hope that you did not know about it."

Goneril entered the courtyard.

King Lear said, "Who comes here? Oh, Heavens, if you love old men, if your sweet rule approves of obedience — the obedience daughters owe to their fathers — if you yourselves are old, make my cause your cause; send down the stored vengeances of Heaven, and take my part!"

He said to Goneril, "Aren't you ashamed to look upon this beard?"

His white beard was a sign of old age and the respect that ought to be accorded to old age.

Regan and Goneril held hands.

King Lear said, "Oh, Regan, will you take her by the hand?"

Goneril replied, "Why shouldn't she take me by the hand, sir? How have I offended you? Not everything is offensive that poor judgment and senility believe to be offensive."

"Oh, sides, you are too tough," King Lear said. "Will you continue to hold my breaking heart inside my chest? How came my servant to be put in the stocks?"

The Duke of Cornwall said, "I set him there, sir, but his disorderly conduct deserved much less good treatment. He should have been punished much more harshly."

"You!" King Lear said. "Did you?"

Regan said, "Please, father, you are weak, and I wish that you would act that way. Return with and stay with my sister until the expiration of your month, and then, after dismissing half your train of followers, come and stay with me. I am now away from home, and I do not have what is needed to take care of and entertain you."

"Return with her to her home, with fifty of my men already dismissed?" King Lear said. "No, rather I abjure all roofs, and choose to wage war against the enmity of the air; to be a comrade with the wolf and owl — to endure the sharp pinch of necessity! Return with her to her home?

"Why, think about the hot-blooded King of France, who took as a wife Cordelia, our youngest born, even without a dowry. I could as well be brought to kneel before his throne, and, like a humble servant, beg for a pension to keep base life afoot. Return with her? Persuade me instead to be a slave and packhorse to this detested servant."

King Lear pointed at Oswald.

"As you choose, sir," Goneril said.

"Please, daughter, do not make me mad," King Lear said. "I will not trouble you, my child. Farewell. We'll meet no more, see one another no more. But yet you are my flesh, my blood, my daughter — or rather you are a disease that's in my flesh, which I must call mine: You are a boil, a plague-sore, a swollen carbuncle, in my disease-corrupted blood. But I'll not criticize you; let shame come to you when it will, I do not call it upon you. I do not bid Jupiter, the thunder-bearer, to shoot bolts of lightning at you, nor do I tell tales of you to Jupiter the highest judge. Mend when you can; be better at your leisure. I can be patient; I can stay with Regan, I and my hundred Knights."

King Lear's Knights had already been reduced to fifty, but he hoped that Regan would honor the agreement made when he gave her dowry to her and allow him to have once more a hundred Knights.

Regan said, "Not so fast. I had not expected you to visit me yet, nor am I prepared with what is necessary to give you a fit welcome. Listen, sir, to my sister. Rational people who listen to your passionate complaints must come to the conclusion that you are old, and so —"

She hesitated and then said, "But she knows what she is doing."

"Is this well spoken?" King Lear asked. "Do you really mean to say this?"

"I dare to say that it is true, sir," Regan replied. "What, fifty followers? Isn't that a good number? Why should you need more? Yes, or so many, since both expense and danger speak against so great a number? To maintain fifty Knights costs much money. And how, in one house, should so many people, under two commands, stay friendly? It is hard, almost impossible, to maintain the peace under such conditions."

Goneril asked, "Why can't you, my lord, be served by those whom she calls her servants or by my own servants?"

"Why not, my lord?" Regan asked. "If then they chanced to slack off while serving you, we could control them. If you will come to me — but now I see danger in you having so many Knights serving you — I entreat you to bring only twenty-five Knights. To no more than that will I give place or recognition."

King Lear said, "I gave you everything —"

"And about time, too," Regan said.

"I made you my guardians and my trustees," King Lear said, "but I reserved some rights. We made an agreement that I would be allowed to have a hundred Knights serving me. What! Must I come to you with only twenty-five Knights, Regan? Don't you remember?"

King Lear had reserved the right to have a hundred Knights serve him as a symbol of his social status. He was a King, not a servant or a beggar.

"If you say that again, my lord, you will have nothing more to do with me," Regan said.

King Lear said, "Wicked creatures look good when they are compared to other creatures that are even more wicked. Not being the worst deserves some praise."

He said to Goneril, "I will go with you. You allow me fifty Knights, and that is double the twenty-five Knights that Regan will allow me to have; therefore, you must love me twice as much as she does."

Goneril said, "Listen to me, my lord. Why do you need twenty-five, ten, or five Knights to serve you in a house where twice so many are commanded to take care of you?"

Regan asked, "Why do you need one Knight?"

King Lear replied, "Oh, reason not the need. Don't ask why they are needed. Even our basest beggars have something more than is absolutely needed. If you were to allow a man no more than what a man absolutely needs, that man's life would be as cheap as a beast's.

"You are a lady, and you wear gorgeous clothing. The purpose of clothing is to keep you warm, and if you have only the clothing that is needed to keep you warm, you would not need the gorgeous clothing you are wearing, which barely keep you warm. You can keep warmer with a plain cloak.

"But, for true need —"

Some things cannot be quantified. King Lear had tried to quantify love by the number of Knights his daughters would allow him, and he had tried to quantify love earlier when before he gave his daughters their dowries he asked them to tell him how much they loved him.

Also, some needs are social. They may not be necessary to keep one alive, but they are nonetheless needs. Such needs include gorgeous clothing and the services of a hundred Knights. They also include love and respect.

King Lear said, "You Heavens, give me patience — the ability to endure pain — that's what I need! You see me here, you gods, a poor old man, as full of grief as of age, and wretched in both!"

He then changed his mind about what he needed: "If you gods are the ones who are stirring these daughters' hearts against their father, don't make me so much a fool that I endure it meekly. Touch me with noble anger, and don't let women's weapons — drops of water, aka tears — stain my man's cheeks!"

He said to Goneril and Regan, "No, you unnatural hags, I will have such revenges on you both, that all the world shall — I will do such things — I don't know what they are yet, but they shall be the terrors of the Earth! You think I'll weep. No, I'll not weep. I have full cause to weep, but this heart shall break into a hundred thousand pieces before I'll weep."

Thunder sounded.

He then said to one of his few supporters, "Oh, Fool, I shall go mad!"

King Lear, the Earl of Gloucester, the disguised Kent, and the Fool left.

The storm started in earnest.

"Let us go inside," the Duke of Cornwall said. "There will be a storm."

Regan said, "This house is little. The old man and his people cannot be well accommodated here."

"It is his own fault," Goneril said. "He has put himself out in the storm and away from shelter, and he has made his mind unrestful and disturbed. He needs to suffer from his folly."

"I'll receive him and take care of him gladly," Regan said, "but not even one of his followers."

"I am resolved to do the same thing," Goneril said. "Where is my lord of Gloucester?"

"He followed the old man," the Duke of Cornwall said. "Here he comes."

The Earl of Gloucester entered the courtyard and said, "The King is in a high rage."

"Where is he going?" the Duke of Cornwall asked.

"He is calling for his horses, but I don't know where he is going."

The Duke of Cornwall said, "It is best to give him his way and let him go. He insists on having his own way."

"My lord, do not ask him to stay," Goneril said.

"The night is coming, and the bleak winds are getting very strong," the Earl of Gloucester said. "There is scarcely even a bush for many miles around here."

Regan said, "Oh, sir, willful men such as my father must learn from the injuries that they inflict on themselves. Shut and lock your doors. My father is served by a desperate train of followers, and since he allows himself to be manipulated by them, wisdom tells us to be afraid of what they may incite him to do."

The Duke of Cornwall, who outranked the Earl of Gloucester, said, "Shut and lock your doors, my lord; it is a wild night. My Regan has given you good advice; come out of the storm."

The Earl of Gloucester did as he was ordered.

# CHAPTER 3
## — 3.1 —

The storm raged on the heath. The disguised Kent and the gentleman, who was another of King Lear's followers, met. The disguised Kent had been separated from King Lear by the storm.

"Who's there, besides foul weather?" the disguised Kent asked.

"One whose mind is like the weather — very unquiet."

"I know who you are," the disguised Kent said. "Where's the King?"

"Struggling against and competing with the raging elements of the storm. He orders the winds to blow the land into the sea or to swell the curled waves above the mainland so that the entire world might change or cease to exist. He tears his white hair, which the impetuous blasts, with blind rage, catch in their fury and show no respect for. He strives in this little world of man to out-scorn the to-and-fro-conflicting wind and rain. In this night, in which the she-bear, whose milk has been emptied by her cubs, would lie in a cave, and in which the lion and the belly-pinched and starving wolf keep their fur dry, he stays outside without a hat and cries out with desperate defiance like a gambler who is betting all he has left."

"But who is with him?" the disguised Kent asked.

"None but the Fool, who labors to outdo the King's heart-struck injuries with extravagant wit."

"Sir, I know your good character, and I dare, because I know that you are a good man, to entrust an important task to you. There is disagreement, although the two are cunning enough to conceal it, between the Duke of Albany and the Duke of Cornwall. They have — and which enthroned great men do not? — servants, who seem to be no other than servants, but who are spies who send to the King of France information about our state. This information includes the quarrels and plots of the two Dukes, or the harsh treatment both Dukes have borne against old and kind King Lear, or something deeper than these things, of which perhaps these other things conceal the truth of what is really going on.

"But it is true that from France an army comes into this divided Kingdom. This army, taking advantage of our negligence, has already gained a secret stronghold in some of our best ports, and the French soldiers are ready to openly show their military banners.

"Now let me tell you what I want you to do. If you trust me enough to dare to speed to Dover, you shall find men there who will thank you for giving an honest report of the unnatural and maddening sorrow that afflicts the King.

"I am a gentleman by birth and education, and because of some reliable information and confidence, I offer you the opportunity to do this service."

The gentleman knew the disguised Kent only as a servant, and so he was skeptical and wanted further information before undertaking this task.

He said, "I will talk further with you."

The disguised Kent knew that the gentleman was skeptical, but he needed the gentleman to quickly go to Dover, and so he needed to quickly give the gentleman enough assurance so the gentleman would quickly leave and do the task.

He said, "No, do not. But for confirmation that I am much more than my outward appearance of a servant suggests, open this wallet, and take the money and ring it contains. If you shall see Cordelia — as you will, don't worry — show her this ring, and she will tell you who your servant — me — is, whom you yet do not know.

"Damn this storm! I will go seek the King."

The gentleman was convinced that the disguised Kent was of a good and high-ranking family. He was willing to undertake the mission.

The gentleman said, "Let's shake hands. Do you have anything else to say to me?"

"Only a few words, but they are more important than all the other words. We need to find the King. You go that way, and I'll go this way. Whoever first finds the King will shout to the other that the King has been found."

In another part of the heath, with the storm still raging, stood King Lear and the Fool.

King Lear shouted into the storm, "Blow, winds! Puff up your cheeks and blow! Rage! Blow! You cataracts — you flood gates of Heaven — and hurricanes, spout water until you have drenched our steeples and drowned the weathercocks! You sulfurous lightning that flashes as quickly as thought, forerunners of thunderbolts that split mighty oaks, singe my white head! And you, all-shaking thunder, smite flat the thick rotundity of the world! Crack Nature's molds and spill all seeds that make ungrateful Humankind!"

The Fool said, "Oh, my uncle, court holy-water in a dry house is better than this rainwater out of doors."

Court holy-water was flattery, something that many courts are known for.

The Fool continued, "My good uncle, go inside, and ask for your daughters' blessing. Here is a night that pities neither wise man nor fool."

The Fool was concerned about the King and wanted him to be somewhere dry and safe, even if it meant apologizing to his daughters.

Ignoring the Fool, King Lear shouted into the storm, "Rumble your bellyful! Spit, fire! Spout, rain! Not rain, nor wind, nor thunder, nor fiery lightning are my daughters. I do not charge you, you elements, with unkindness toward me. I never gave you a Kingdom, and I never called you my children. You owe me no allegiance, and so let fall on me your horrible pleasure. Here I stand, your slave: a poor, infirm, weak, and despised old man. But yet I call you servile agents that have with two pernicious daughters joined your Heavenly armies against a head as old and white as this. Oh! Oh! It is foul!"

The Fool said, "He who has a house to put his head in has a good head-piece."

The compound word "head-piece" meant both a helmet and a brain.

The Fool sang this song:

*"The cod-piece that will house*

*"Before the head has any,*

*"The head and he shall louse;*

*"So beggars marry many."*

The compound word "cod-piece" meant "penis" in this context.

The Fool was saying that a penis that sought a home — vagina — before the head had a home would suffer. Both the head hair and the pubic hair would be infested with lice. Someone who was impudent and sought sex rather than love would end up a beggar and would "marry" — be joined with — many lice.

The Fool then sang this song:

*"The man who makes his toe*

*"What he his heart should make*

*"Shall of a corn, aka bunion on a toe, cry woe,*

*"And turn his sleep to wake."*

This meant that the man who treasures something trivial such as a toe rather than something precious such as his heart would end up hurting and unable to sleep at night.

King Lear had done this. He had valued Goneril and Regan more than he had valued Cordelia.

The Fool was not trying to cheer up King Lear. Instead of being funny, the Fool's words were wise. King Lear was in the process of learning from his mistakes, but he had not learned all that he needed to learn. He had learned that Goneril and Regan were bad daughters, but he still needed to learn to value Cordelia, although he had started the process of doing that.

The Fool then said, "For there was never yet a beautiful woman who did not make mouths when she looked in a mirror."

The phrase "make mouths" meant to "make faces." A beautiful woman could smile when she looked in a mirror to make herself more beautiful, but to "make a mouth" could also mean to make a contemptuous smile, such as the one that Oswald gave the disguised Kent before the disguised Kent was put in the stocks.

Cordelia might smile pleasantly when she looked in a mirror, but Goneril and Regan were very capable of making contemptuous smiles when looking into a mirror — looking at the face of a close relative can be like looking into a mirror. In fact, they smiled when they recently took their father's Knights away from him. It is possible to infuriate an old father by saying hurtful words in a soothing voice.

King Lear calmed down and said, "No, I will be the pattern of all patience and self-control. I will say nothing."

The disguised Kent came out of the darkness and asked, "Who's there?"

The Fool replied, "Here's grace and a cod-piece; that's a wise man and a fool."

The Fool did not say who was the wise man and who was the fool.

The disguised Kent said to King Lear, "Alas, sir, are you here? Things that love night do not love such nights as these; the wrathful skies frighten the very wanderers of the dark and make them stay in their caves. Ever since I became a man, I cannot remember ever experiencing such a storm as this: such sheets of fire, such bursts of horrible thunder, such groans of roaring wind and rain. Man's nature cannot endure the affliction of the storm or the fear it inspires."

King Lear said, "Let the great gods, who keep this dreadful tumult over our heads, find out who are their enemies now. Tremble, you wretches, who have within you secret crimes, unpunished by justice. Hide yourselves, you bloody murderers, you perjurers, and you incestuous men who pretend to be virtuous. Tremble, wretches who under secret and convenient appearances have plotted against the lives of men. Well-concealed criminals, burst out of your concealing hiding places, and cry for mercy from these dreadful summoners who wish to see you punished."

A summoner was a man who took an accused person to an ecclesiastical court to be tried.

King Lear paused and then added, "I am a man who is more sinned against than sinning."

The disguised Kent said, "I am sorry to see you bare-headed in this storm! My gracious lord, nearby here is a hovel; it will lend you some friendship and protection against the tempest. Rest there while I go to this hard house, the inhabitants of which — your daughters — are harder than the stones of which the house is made. Just now, your daughters, when I was asking about you and your whereabouts, refused to let me in. Let me return there and force them to show some courtesy to you, their father."

King Lear said, "My wits begin to turn."

His mind was changing; he was growing and beginning to be empathetic. Just a while ago, he had been calling for the extinction of Humankind, but now he began to be concerned about the man — or perhaps boy — who was his Fool. He wanted shelter for the Fool.

He said to the Fool, "Come on, my boy. How are you doing, my boy? Are you cold? I am cold myself."

He said to the disguised Kent, "Where is this straw, my servant? Necessity has strange powers and can make vile things — such as warm straw in a hovel — precious. Come, take us to the hovel you have found."

He said to his Fool, "Poor Fool and knave, I still have one part in my heart that is alive and feels empathy for you."

The Fool sang this song:

*"He who has a little tiny wit —*

*"With hey, ho, the wind and the rain —*

*"Must make happiness with his fortunes fit,*

*"For the rain it rains every day."*

This song meant that a person who is not very intelligent — a description that applies to all of us — must find a way to be happy with life despite the rain, aka evil, that falls upon each of us continually.

King Lear said to the Fool, "True, my good boy."

He then said to the disguised Kent, "Come, take us to this hovel."

King Lear and the disguised Kent departed, and the Fool said this to you, the reader:

"This is a splendid night to cool the lust of a courtesan — on such a night she won't be horny."

He paused and then added, "I'll tell you a prophecy before I go:

"When priests are more in word than matter,

"In other words, when priests talk more about sin than actually commit sin,

"Or perhaps, in other words, when priests talk more about leading an ethical life than actually try to lead an ethical life,

"When brewers mar their malt with water,

"In other words, when brewers water their beer and make it healthier and decrease alcoholism,

"Or perhaps, in other words, when brewers ruin their beer by watering it down,

"When nobles are their tailors' tutors,

"In other words, when nobles know how to do the work of the common people,

"Or perhaps, in other words, when nobles think they know more than the real experts know,

"When no heretics are burned, except wenches' suitors,

"In other words, when no heretics are burned, except women's suitors, who are properly punished as they burn from venereal disease because they did not obey the word of God,

"When every case in law is right,

"In other words, when no innocent people are convicted and no guilty people remain unpunished,

"When no squire is in debt, nor no poor Knight,

"In other words, when people stay out of debt,

"When slanders do not live in tongues,

"In other words, when people do not spread malicious gossip,

"Nor cutpurses come not to throngs,

"In other words, when pickpockets do not go among crowds of people and steal,

"When usurers tell their gold in the field,

"In other words, when moneylenders count their money in the open,

"And bawds and whores do churches build,

"In other words, when panderers and whores turn to God and build churches,

"Then shall the realm of Albion

"In other words, then shall the realm of England

"Come to great confusion,

"In other words, England shall be troubled,

"And then comes the time, who lives to see it,

"In other words, and then comes the time, whoever lives to see it,

"That going shall be used with feet.

"In other words, then walking shall be done with feet."

This prophecy stated that England would always be troubled — even if it were a utopia.

Of course, a utopia will never happen in the real world, and because it will never happen (and even if it did happen), England will continue to be troubled.

What is a sure way to tell that England is troubled? If men walk with their feet, then you know that England is troubled.

It does not matter whether you are an optimist or a pessimist, England is troubled.

The Fool then said, "This prophecy Merlin shall make; for I live before his time."

The Fool and King Lear lived centuries before the time of Merlin and King Arthur and the Knights of the Round Table, but the prophecy was true at the time that King Lear lived, and it was true at the time that Merlin lived.

It is still true today.

It will always be true until Humankind becomes extinct.

What the prophecy says about England is true of the world as a whole.

The Earl of Gloucester and his illegitimate son, Edmund, spoke together in a room in his castle.

"It's sad, Edmund. I do not like this unnatural treatment of fathers. When I asked for permission from the Duke of Cornwall, Regan, and Goneril to show pity to and help King Lear, they took from me the use of my own house and they ordered me, on pain of their perpetual displeasure with me, not to speak of him, entreat for him, or in any way sustain and help him."

"This is very savage and unnatural!" Edmund said.

"Quiet!" the Earl of Gloucester said. "You must say nothing about that; it's dangerous. In addition, there's a division between the Dukes, and a worse matter than that. I have received a letter tonight; it is dangerous to speak about that, too. I have locked the letter in my private room. These injuries the King now bears will be fully revenged. Part of an army has already landed; we must be on the side of the King. I will leave and seek him, and secretly help him. You go and talk with the Duke of Cornwall to keep him occupied so that he does not learn about my charity. If he asks for me, tell him that I am ill and have gone to bed.

"Even if I die because of it — and they have threatened to do no less to me — the King my old master must be helped.

"Strange things are happening, Edmund; please be careful."

He exited.

Alone, Edmund said to himself, "This act of charity, which you have been forbidden to do, I shall immediately tell the Duke of Cornwall about, and I will tell him about that letter, too.

"These acts will deserve a reward from the Duke of Cornwall, and I will win what my father loses — that will be everything. The younger rises when the old does fall."

On the heath in front of the hovel stood King Lear, the disguised Kent, and the Fool. The storm continued to rage.

The disguised Kent said, "Here is the place, my lord. My good lord, enter the hovel. The tyranny of the night in the open air is too rough for human nature to endure."

King Lear replied, "Let me alone."

The disguised Kent repeated, "My good lord, enter the hovel."

"Do you want to break my heart?"

"I had rather break my own," Kent replied. "My good lord, enter the hovel."

"You think it is much that this contentious storm invades us to the skin with wind and water," King Lear said. "So it is much to you, but wherever the greater malady is fixed, the lesser is scarcely felt. You would prefer to run away from a bear, but if your flight lay toward the raging sea, you would face the bear head-on. When the mind is free and unburdened, the body's delicate. The tempest in my mind takes all feeling from my senses — except the tempest beating there. Because of the mental pain I feel for my daughters' ingratitude, I cannot feel any physical pain brought by this storm. Filial ingratitude! Isn't it as if this mouth should bite this hand because it lifts food to it? But I will punish them thoroughly."

He hesitated and said, "No, I will weep no more. On such a night they shut me out of doors! Pour on the pain and the rain; I will endure them. On such a night as this! Oh, Regan, Goneril! Your old kind father, whose generous heart gave you everything — oh, that way madness lies, so let me not think of that. No more of that."

Worried about King Lear, the disguised Kent again said, "My good lord, enter the hovel."

"Please, go in yourself," King Lear replied. "Seek your own comfort. My being outside in this tempest will not allow me to think about things that would hurt me more. But I'll go in."

He said to the Fool, "In, boy; you go in first."

He thought about other poor people outside on this night and said, "You homeless poor —"

Then he said to the Fool, who was waiting for him, "No, you go in first. I'll pray, and then I'll sleep."

The Fool went inside the hovel. The disguised Kent stayed outside with King Lear.

King Lear said, "Poor naked wretches, wherever you are, who endure the pelting of this pitiless storm, how shall your homeless heads and unfed bellies, and your ragged clothing filled with holes defend you from weather such as this?"

He then blamed himself for not caring more about the poor when he had wealth and power: "Oh, I have been too little concerned about this! Take this medicine, pompous people: Expose yourself so that you feel what poor wretches feel, and you will learn to give the excess of your wealth to them, and show the Heavens how wealth can be more fairly distributed."

Edgar, now disguised as a Tom o'Bedlam, said in a disguised voice from inside the hovel, where he had taken shelter, "Fathom and a half! Fathom and a half! Poor Tom!"

A fathom is six feet of water. The disguised Edgar was speaking as if he were a sailor taking soundings — measuring the depth of water — in a sinking ship.

The Fool ran out of the hovel.

"Don't go in there, my uncle," he cried. "There's a supernatural spirit inside. Help me! Help me!"

The disguised Kent said, "Give me your hand. Who's there?"

The Fool replied, "A spirit — a supernatural spirit. He says his name's poor Tom."

The disguised Kent yelled, "Who are you who mumbles there in the straw? Come outside."

Edgar, disguised as a mad man, came outside. He was naked except for a blanket around his waist. He was dirty and his hair was matted, and he had pushed thorns into his arms.

The disguised Edgar, pretending to believe that the Devil tormented him, said, "Stay away! The foul fiend follows me! Through the sharp hawthorn blows the cold wind. You are cold — go to your beds, and warm yourselves."

King Lear asked him, "Have you given everything to your two daughters? Is that why you have come to this?"

The disguised Edgar replied, "Who gives anything to poor Tom? He is the man whom the foul fiend has led through fire and through flame, and through ford and whirlpool and over bog and quagmire. The foul fiend has tempted poor Tom to commit suicide. He has laid knives under his pillow, and put hangman's ropes in his church pew, and set rat poison by his soup. The foul fiend has made him proud of heart, and the foul fiend has made him ride on a bay trotting-horse over four-inch-wide bridges in order to chase his own shadow as if it were a traitor. May God bless your five wits! Tom's a-cold."

The disguised Edgar shivered and said, "May God bless and protect you from whirlwinds, the influences of evil stars, and infection! Do poor Tom some charity — poor Tom whom the foul fiend vexes."

The disguised Edgar pretended to fight an invisible demon, saying, "There could I have him now — and there — and there again, and there."

The storm continued to rage.

King Lear asked, "What, have his daughters brought him to this distress?"

He asked the disguised Edgar, "Couldn't you save anything and keep it for yourself? Did you give them everything?"

The Fool said, "No, he reserved a blanket, else we had been all embarrassed at seeing his bare butt."

King Lear had reserved for himself the services of a hundred Knights.

In this society, people believed that diseases hung in the air, waiting until they were poured out to inflict pain on human beings.

King Lear said, "Now, may all the plagues that in the pendulous air hang fated over men's faults fall and alight on your daughters!"

The disguised Kent said, "He has no daughters, sir."

"Death to you, traitor!" King Lear shouted. "Nothing could have brought this human to such lowness but his unkind daughters. Is it the fashion that discarded and cast-off fathers should have thus little mercy on their flesh?"

He was looking at the thorns in the disguised Edgar's arms, but he could also have been thinking of the thorns in his own mind.

He said, "Judicious punishment! It was this flesh that begot those pelican daughters."

In this society, people believed that the young of pelicans would bite the breast of their parents and feed on the blood that flowed from the wound.

Hearing the word "pelican," the disguised Edgar said, "Pillicock sat on Pillicock-hill."

A 'Pillicock" was a cutesy name for a penis, and a "Pillicock-hill" was a cutesy name for a vulva.

The disguised Edgar then sang, "Halloo, halloo, loo, loo!"

The Fool said seriously, "This cold night will turn us all to fools and madmen."

The disguised Edgar said, "Take heed of the foul fiend. Obey your parents. Keep true to your word. Do not swear. Do not commit adultery with a man's sworn spouse. Do not set your sweet heart on fancy clothing. Tom's a-cold."

King Lear asked him, "What have you been?"

The disguised Edgar replied, "A serving-man, proud in heart and mind. I was a courier. I curled my hair. I wore gloves — favors from my mistress — in my cap. I served the lust of my mistress' heart, and I did the act of darkness with her. I swore as many oaths as I spoke words, and I broke them openly in the sweet face of Heaven. I was a man who dreamed of lustful acts as he slept and then woke up and did them. Wine I loved deeply, dice and gambling I loved dearly, and when it came to women I had more mistresses than the Turkish Sultan. I was false of heart, light of ear and ready to believe malicious gossip, and bloody of hand. I was like a hog when it came to sloth, a fox when it came to stealth, a wolf when it came to greediness, a dog when it came to madness, and a lion when it came to hunting of prey.

"You may be tempted by the creaking of fashionable shoes and the rustling of the silk clothing of a woman as she meets a lover in a secret assignation, but do not betray your poor heart to that woman. Keep your feet out of brothels, keep your hands out of the openings of petticoats, keep your signature away from contracts in which you borrow money, and defy the foul fiend."

The disguised Edgar then sang these words:

"*Still through the hawthorn blows the cold wind:*

"*Says suum, mun, ha, no, nonny.*

"*Dauphin, my boy, my boy, sessa! Be quiet! Let him trot by.*"

The Dauphin was the son of a King of France, and Edgar was singing a combination of an old ballad and nonsense syllables. In the old ballad, the King of France wanted the Dauphin to be safe and not gain a reputation for valor by combating a notable opponent during wartime. Every time a notable opponent rode by, the King of France would tell his son, the Dauphin, "Be quiet! Let him trot by." In Edgar's version of the ballad, the Dauphin was not even allowed to combat the cold wind because it was too dangerous.

The storm continued to rage.

King Lear said to the disguised Edgar, "Why, you would be better off in your grave than to confront with your naked and uncovered body this extreme severity of the skies."

He then said to the disguised Kent and to the Fool, "Is man no more than this? Look carefully at him."

He said to the disguised Edgar, "You owe the worm no silk, the beast no hide, the sheep no wool, the cat no perfume."

The disguised Edgar was naked. He did not wear silk or leather or woolen clothing. He also did not wear perfume made from the musk of the civet cat.

King Lear continued, "Ha! The three of us — my servant, the Fool, and me — are wearing clothing. We have disguised our nakedness. You are the natural man himself: a man without the trappings of civilization is no more than such a poor bare, forked-legged animal as you are."

He started to tear off his clothing, saying, "Off, off, you trappings of civilization! Come! I will unbutton my clothing here."

The Fool said, "Please, my uncle, control yourself; it is an evil night to go swimming in. Now a little fire in a wild field would be like an old lecher's heart: a small spark — all the rest of his body would be cold. Look, here comes a walking fire."

The Earl of Gloucester, carrying a torch, walked up to them.

The disguised Edgar said, "This is the foul fiend Flibbertigibbet: he begins at curfew, and walks till the first cock; from dusk to dawn he walks. He gives the web and the pin, aka eye cataracts. He makes the eye squint, and he makes the harelip. He mildews the white wheat that is almost ready for harvest, and he hurts the poor creatures of Earth."

He then sang this song as protection against the "evil spirit":

*"Saint Withold footed thrice the wold,*

*"In other words, Saint Withold went three times around the upland plains,*

*"He met the nightmare, and her nine-fold,*

*"In other words, he met the demon called the nightmare, which sits on the chests of sleeping people and makes it hard for them to breathe, and he met her nine followers,*

*"Bid her alight,*

*"In other words, he ordered her to get off the chest of the sleeper,*

*"And her troth plight,*

*"In other words, and swear to do no more harm,*

*"And, 'Aroint you, witch, aroint you!'*

*"In other words, and said, 'Leave, witch, leave!'"*

The disguised Kent said to King Lear, "How is your grace?"

King Lear asked about the man with the torch, "Who is he?"

"Who's there?" the disguised Kent said. "What is it you want?"

The Earl of Gloucester asked, "Who are you there? What are your names?"

The disguised Edgar replied, "Poor Tom, who eats the swimming frog, the toad, the tadpole, the wall-lizard, and the water-newt. Poor Tom, who in the fury of his heart, when the foul fiend rages, eats cow-dung for salads, swallows the old rat and the dead dog in the ditch, drinks the green scum of the stagnant pond. Poor Tom, who is whipped from parish to parish, who is put in stocks, and who is imprisoned. Poor Tom, who used to have three suits to his back, six shirts to his body, a horse to ride, and a weapon to wear. But mice and rats, and such small animals, have been Tom's food for seven long years. Beware the demon who follows me. Peace, Smulkin; peace, you fiend!"

"What, has your grace no better company?" the Earl of Gloucester asked King Lear.

The disguised Edgar said, "The Prince of Darkness is a gentleman. Modo he's called, and Mahu."

The Earl of Gloucester said, "Our flesh and blood, aka children, are grown so vile, my lord, that it hates what begets it."

The disguised Edgar said, "Poor Tom's a-cold."

The Earl of Gloucester said to King Lear, "Go inside one of my buildings with me. I must do my duty; I cannot endure to obey all of your daughters' hard commands. Although they have ordered me to bar my doors and let this tyrannous night take hold upon you, yet I have ventured to find you and bring you where both fire and food are ready."

King Lear said to the Earl of Gloucester about the disguised Edgar, whom the Earl of Gloucester did not recognize as being his own son, "First let me talk with this natural philosopher."

He asked the disguised Edgar, "What is the cause of thunder?"

In his madness, King Lear thought that the disguised Edgar was an educated man and a natural philosopher, aka a person who investigated Nature.

The disguised Kent said, "My good lord, take his offer; go into the house."

King Lear replied, "I'll talk a word with this same learned Theban."

The ancient Greeks, including those from Thebes and Athens, were thought to be wise.

King Lear asked the disguised Edgar, "What is your main area of study?"

The disguised Edgar replied, "How to thwart the fiend, and to kill vermin."

King Lear said, "Let me ask you one word in private."

The disguised Kent said to the Earl of Gloucester, "Importune him once more to go, my lord. His mind has begun to become unsettled."

"Can you blame him?" the Earl of Gloucester replied.

The storm continued to rage.

The Earl of Gloucester continued, "King Lear's daughters seek his death. Ah, I remember the Earl of Kent! He was a good man. He, poor banished man, predicted it would be like this! You say the King grows mad; I'll tell you, friend, I am almost mad myself. I had a son, who is now an outlaw whom I have disinherited. He sought my life just recently — very recently. I loved him, friend; no father ever loved his son dearer. I tell you the truth: The grief has crazed my wits. What a night's this!"

He said to King Lear, "I do beg your grace —"

King Lear interrupted and said, "I beg your pardon," and then he went back to talking to the disguised Edgar, "Noble philosopher, I desire your company."

The disguised Edgar replied, "Tom's a-cold."

The Earl of Gloucester, who did not intend to help the Tom o'Bedlam, said to him, "Go in, fellow, there, into the hovel. Keep yourself warm there."

King Lear said, "Come, let's all go in."

The disguised Kent said, "This way, my lord."

He wanted King Lear to go away from the hovel and to the building that the Earl of Gloucester had offered as shelter.

King Lear put an arm around the disguised Edgar's shoulders and said, "I will go with him. I will stay always with my philosopher."

The disguised Kent said, "My good lord, humor the King; let him take the fellow with him."

"You accompany the fellow," the Earl of Gloucester said.

The disguised Kent said to the disguised Edgar, "Sirrah, come on; you can go along with us."

King Lear said to the disguised Edgar, "Come, good Athenian."

The ancient Athenians included many philosophers.

The Earl of Gloucester said to King Lear, "No words, no words. Hush."

Edgar sang these words:

"*Child Roland to the dark tower came,*

"*His motto was always this — Fie, foh, and fum,*

"*I smell the blood of a British man.*"

A "child" was a candidate for Knighthood, and child Roland was the nephew of Charlemagne and the hero of the epic poem *The Song of Roland*. The disguised Edgar was pretending to confuse Roland with the giant in the fairy tale "Jack and the Beanstalk." Much real confusion was happening in Britain.

In the Earl of Gloucester's castle, the Duke of Cornwall and Edmund, the Earl of Gloucester's deceitful and illegitimate son, were talking. As Edmund had promised himself he would do, he had informed the Duke of Cornwall that the Earl of Gloucester, Edmund's father, had — against orders — gone to help King Lear. Edmund had also searched for and found the letter that his father had received about the invasion of the French army.

The Duke of Cornwall said, "I will have my revenge before I leave his house."

Edmund replied, "My lord, I am afraid to think of how I may be criticized because my natural affection for my father is thus giving way to my loyalty to you, my lord."

The Duke of Cornwall said, "I now realize that it was not altogether your brother Edgar's evil disposition that made him seek your father's death. Also a factor was the Earl of Gloucester's own evil disposition that deserved to be punished with death. That and your brother's evil disposition made your brother want to kill your father."

Edmund said, "How malicious is my fortune, that I must repent my being just! I did the right thing when I informed you about my father's evil, but I feel bad because I informed against my own father. This is the letter he spoke about, which proves that he was a spy who sent information to France. Oh, Heavens! I wish that this treason had never occurred, or that I was not the person who detected it!"

"Go with me to the Duchess Regan," the Duke of Cornwall said.

Edmund replied, "If the content of this paper is true, you have mighty business at hand."

"True or false, it has made you the new Earl of Gloucester. You now take your father's title. Find out where your father is, so that he can be arrested."

Edmund thought, *If I find him comforting the King, it will make the Duke of Cornwall even more suspicious.*

He said out loud to the Duke of Cornwall, "I will persevere in my course of loyalty, although the conflict between my loyalty to you and my loyalty to my father is sharp."

"I will trust in you, and you will find me to be a dearer father than your biological father in my love for you."

In a room in a farmhouse near the castle were the old Earl of Gloucester, King Lear, the disguised Kent, the Fool, and Edgar, who was still disguised as a Tom o'Bedlam. The old Earl of Gloucester did not yet know that his illegitimate son, Edmund, had become the new Earl of Gloucester.

"This place here is better than the open air," the old Earl of Gloucester said. "Take it thankfully. I will supplement the comfort with what additions I can. I will do what I can to make this place more comfortable for you. I will not be long away from you."

The disguised Kent replied quietly, "All the power of King Lear's wits have given way to his suffering and his anger. He is insane."

He then said loudly to the old Earl of Gloucester, "May the gods reward your kindness!"

The old Earl of Gloucester departed.

The disguised Edgar said, "Frateretto calls to me, and he tells me that the Roman Emperor Nero is an angler in the lake of darkness."

He then said to the Fool, "Pray, innocent, and beware the foul fiend."

The Fool said to King Lear, "Please, my uncle, tell me whether a madman is a gentleman or a yeoman."

A gentleman has a higher social status than a yeoman. A gentleman has a coat of arms; a yeoman owns land but has no coat of arms.

King Lear replied, "A King! A King!"

The Fool replied, "No, a madman is a yeoman who has a gentleman as his son because he's a mad yeoman who sees his son become a gentleman before he does."

This was a cynical view. Loving fathers are happy to see their sons do better than they themselves did and advance in society and in life, but in the Fool's joke this father was not happy to see his son do better than he did.

Of course, in loving families, family members are happy to see other family members do well, but Goneril and Regan were happy to see their aged father combat the storm although they could easily shelter him.

King Lear thought about the punishment his two daughters deserved, and he said out loud, "To have a thousand with red burning spits come hissing in upon them —"

The thousand could be devils if the two daughters were punished in Hell.

The disguised Edgar said, "The foul fiend bites my back."

The Fool said, "He's a madman who trusts in the tameness of a wolf, a horse's health, a boy's love, or a whore's oath."

This was more cynicism from the Fool. Yes, a "tame" wolf may bite, a horse's health may decline or be lied about, and a whore may lie. But is a father a madman if he believes that his son loves him? Are all sons like Edmund?

King Lear, still lost in a fantasy world, came up with the idea of putting Goneril and Regan on trial.

He said, "It shall be done; I will immediately bring them to trial."

He said to the disguised Edgar, "Come, you sit here, most learned justice."

He said to the Fool, "You, wise sir, sit here."

He then said to the air, "Now, you she-foxes!"

The disguised Edgar said about King Lear, "Look, where he stands and glares!"

He then said to the air, "Do you want eyes looking at you at your trial, madam?"

He sang, "*Come over the bourn, Bessie, to me —*"

The word "bourn" meant "stream."

The Fool sang these words:

"*Her boat has a leak,*

"*And she must not speak*

"*Why she dares not come over to you.*"

The Fool's words had a double meaning. The woman's period had started, and she did not want to tell her lover why she would not cross the stream to be with him.

The Fool's jokes, if you can call them jokes, were now usually about breakdowns or difficulties in personal relationships. This time, the difficulty was not nearly as serious as two daughters wishing their father to be killed. However, the Fool's song did involve sex between unmarried partners. A husband tends to know when his wife is on her period.

When things go wrong at the top — when a King is badly treated — things go wrong at other levels of society.

The disguised Edgar said, "The foul fiend haunts poor Tom in the voice of a nightingale."

The disguised Edgar was pretending that the foul fiend was the Fool, who had a good singing voice.

He continued, "Hopdance cries in Tom's belly for two white unsmoked herring. Croak and rumble not, black angel. I have no food for you."

His belly was growling from hunger.

The disguised Kent was more concerned about King Lear than about the disguised Edgar's hunger, and he said to King Lear, "How are you, sir? Don't stand there looking so dumbfounded. Will you lie down and rest upon the cushions?"

King Lear said, "I'll see their trial first. Bring in the evidence."

He said to the disguised Edgar, "You robed man of justice, take your place."

To King Lear, the disguised Edgar's blanket was now a judicial robe.

King Lear then said to the Fool, "And you, his partner in justice, sit on the bench by his side."

He said to the disguised Kent, "You are on the judicial commission, so you sit down, too."

The disguised Edgar said, "Let us be just."

He sang this song:

*"Are you asleep or awake, jolly shepherd?*

*"Your sheep are in the corn;*

*"And if you give just one blast of your delicate mouth,*

*"Your sheep shall take no harm."*

Enterotoxemia is a severe and sometimes fatal disease of sheep that is caused by a sudden increase of grain in the sheep's diet. Grain is good for sheep when eaten in the right amount, but too much grain can kill sheep.

In Edgar's song, the shepherd needs to take care of his sheep and not allow them to eat too much grain. If the shepherd blows on his horn, help will arrive to get the sheep out of the field of grain. This is good for the sheep and good for the owner of the grain. Moderation is important.

King Lear had given his older daughters too much power and wealth too quickly. It had changed and harmed them. He had been a bad shepherd.

The disguised Edgar then said, "Purr! The cat is gray."

He may have been referring to a demon in the form of a grey cat that he pretended to see.

King Lear said, "Arraign her first; bring Goneril here before the court to answer a criminal charge."

He then said, "I here take my oath before this honorable assembly and say that she kicked the poor King her father."

The Fool said, "Come hither, mistress. Is your name Goneril?"

King Lear said, "She cannot deny it."

The Fool said, "I beg your pardon. I mistook you for a stool."

Of course, Goneril was not present — just the stool that she would have been sitting on.

King Lear then said about Regan, "And here's another, whose warped and distorted looks proclaim what kind of material her heart is made of. Stop her there! She is trying to escape! Arms! Arms! Sword! Fire! Corruption is in the place! She bribed someone to allow her to escape!"

He said to the disguised Edgar, "False justice, why have you let her escape?"

Shocked, the disguised Edgar replied, "Bless your five wits!"

The disguised Kent said, "I feel pity."

He said to King Lear, "Sir, where are your patience and self-control now, which you so often have boasted to possess?"

The disguised Edgar thought, *My tears begin to trickle because I pity King Lear so much — they will ruin my disguise.*

King Lear said about imaginary dogs, "The little dogs and all — their names are Tray, Blanch, and Sweetheart — see, they bark at me."

He imagined that even small pet dogs had turned against him.

The disguised Edgar said, "Tom will throw his head back like a howling dog and yell at them:

"Avaunt, you curs! Get out!

"Whether your mouth be black or white,

"Tooth that poisons if it bite;

"Mastiff, greyhound, mongrel grim,

"Hound or spaniel, brach-bitch or him,

"Whether bobtail short or very long tail,

"Tom will make them weep and wail:

"For, with throwing back thus my head and howling,

"Dogs leap over the bottom piece of a two-piece door, and all are fled."

He yelled and then said, "*Sessa*! Quiet! Come, march to wakes and fairs and market towns. These are good places for begging. Poor Tom, your begging horn is empty."

The disguised Edgar was hungry, but everyone was concerned about King Lear, not Tom o'Bedlam. King Lear was insane and unable to recognize that the disguised Edgar was hungry.

King Lear said, "Then let them dissect Regan to see what grows about her heart. Is there any cause in nature that makes these hard hearts?"

He said to the disguised Edgar, "You, sir, I employ as one of my hundred Knights; however, I do not like the fashion of your garments. You will say that they are luxurious Persian attire, but let them be changed for something more to my liking."

The disguised Kent said to King Lear, "Now, my good lord, lie here and rest awhile."

King Lear, thinking that he was in a four-post bed with curtains, said, "Make no noise, make no noise; draw the curtains. So, so, so. We'll eat our evening meal in the morning. So, so, so."

He needed rest more than he needed food.

The Fool said, "And I'll go to bed at noon."

The old Earl of Gloucester entered the room and said to the disguised Kent, "Come here, friend. Where is my master the King?"

"Here, sir, but do not bother him; his wits are gone and he is insane."

"Good friend, I beg you, take the King in your arms. I have overheard a plot of death against him. A vehicle and a stretcher are ready; lay him in the vehicle, and drive him to Dover, friend, where you will find both welcome and protection. Pick up your master, put him in the stretcher, and carry him to the vehicle. If you should delay even half an hour, his life, and your life, and the lives of all who offer to defend him, will certainly be lost. Pick him up! Pick him up and follow me. I will quickly take you to the vehicle, which has provisions for your journey."

The disguised Kent said, "The King's oppressed brain sleeps."

He then spoke as if he were speaking to the sleeping King, "This much-needed rest might yet have healed your broken senses, which, if circumstances will not allow you to continue to rest, it will be difficult to cure."

The disguised Kent said to the Fool, "Come, help to carry your master. You must not stay behind."

The old Earl of Gloucester said, "Hurry! Hurry!"

Everyone left the disguised Edgar, who would not go with King Lear to Dover.

Alone, the disguised Edgar said, "When we see our betters bearing the same kind of woes we have, we scarcely think our miseries are our foes. A person who suffers by himself suffers most in the mind, leaving carefree things and happy scenes behind. But when grief has fellow sufferers, it skips over much suffering. How light and bearable my pain seems now, when that which makes me bend makes the King bow — he suffers much more than I do. He suffers unjustly because of his children; I suffer unjustly because of my father. Tom o'Bedlam — that is, me — let's go away! Listen to the rumors of differences between those in power. Tom o'Bedlam can reveal himself to be Edgar when misconceptions, which now greatly defile you, are proven to be wrong. At that time, your status as an outlaw will be repealed and you will be reconciled to your father. Whatever else will happen tonight, may King Lear escape safely! In the meanwhile, I must stay hidden."

# — 3.7 —

The Duke of Cornwall, Regan, Goneril, and Edmund, along with some servants, were in a room in the Earl of Gloucester's castle.

The Duke of Cornwall said to Goneril, "Ride quickly to the Duke of Albany, your husband. Show him this letter that was sent to the old Earl of Gloucester; it states that the army of France has landed here in Britain."

He then ordered, "Find the old Earl of Gloucester, who is a villain."

Some of the servants exited.

Regan said about the old Earl of Gloucester, "Hang him immediately."

Goneril said, "Pluck out his eyes."

The Duke of Cornwall said, "Leave him to my displeasure. Edmund, you keep our sister-in-law company during your journey; go with Goneril because the revenges we are determined to take against your traitorous father are not fit for you to see."

He then said to Goneril, "Advise the Duke of Albany, when you see him, to quickly prepare for war. We will do the same. Our posts back and forth between us shall be swift and full of information. Farewell, dear sister-in-law; farewell, my new Earl of Gloucester."

Oswald entered the room.

The Duke of Cornwall asked, "Where is King Lear?"

Oswald replied, "My old Earl of Gloucester has conveyed him away from here. Some thirty-five or -six of the King's Knights, who were urgently seeking for him, met him at the gate. These Knights, along with some other lords who serve King Lear, have gone with him toward Dover, where they claim to have well-armed friends."

The Duke of Cornwall ordered, "Get horses for your mistress."

Goneril said to the Duke of Cornwall and Regan, "Farewell, sweet lord, and sister."

The Duke of Cornwall said, "Edmund, farewell."

Goneril, Edmund, and Oswald exited.

The Duke of Cornwall ordered, "Go seek the traitor: the old Earl of Gloucester. Tie him up like a thief, and bring him before us."

Some servants exited.

The Duke of Cornwall said, "Although we may not execute him without a trial, yet our power shall do a favor for our wrath. Men may criticize what we do, but they cannot stop me from doing it."

He heard a noise and said, "Who's there? The traitor?"

The old Earl of Gloucester entered the room, under guard.

Regan said, "Ungrateful fox! It is he."

The servants had not obeyed all of the Duke of Cornwall's orders; they had not tied up the old Earl of Gloucester.

The Duke of Cornwall ordered, "Bind fast his old and withered arms."

The servants did not act immediately.

"What do your graces intend to do to me?" the old Earl of Gloucester asked. "My good friends, remember that you are my guests; do no foul play to me, friends."

The castle belonged to the Earl of Gloucester. He was the host, and the Duke of Cornwall and Regan were his guests. Ever since ancient times, to harm a host has been acknowledged to be an evil deed. An important theme of Homer's *Odyssey* is the relationship between hosts and guests, and the Trojan War was fought over a violation of that relationship: Paris, a Prince of Troy who was the guest of King Menelaus of Sparta, ran away with Helen, Menelaus' wife. Helen became known as Helen of Troy. In Dante's *Inferno*, guests who harmed hosts, and hosts who harmed guests, are punished in the lowest circle of hell; this shows how serious a sin these violations of trust are.

The Duke of Cornwall said, "Bind him, I say."

Some servants bound the old Earl of Gloucester.

Regan said, "Bind him tightly — tightly. Oh, filthy traitor!"

The old Earl of Gloucester said, "Unmerciful lady as you are, I am not a traitor."

The Duke of Cornwall ordered, "Bind him to this chair. Villain, you shall find —"

Regan plucked some hairs from the old Earl of Gloucester's beard. This was a serious insult.

The old Earl of Gloucester said, "By the kind gods, to pluck some hairs out of my beard is a very ignoble act."

Regan said, "Your beard is so white! You ought to be wise! How can you be such a traitor!"

"Evil lady, these hairs that you pull from my chin will come to life and accuse you of sin: I am your host, and you ought not to do violence to your host's face with your robbers' hands. What will you do with me?"

The Duke of Cornwall asked, "Sir, what letters have you recently received from France?"

"Give a straight answer," Regan said, "because we know the truth."

The Duke of Cornwall asked, "And what conspiracy have you formed with the traitors who have recently landed in the Kingdom?"

Regan asked, "To whom have you sent the lunatic King? Speak."

The old Earl of Gloucester said, "I have a letter that contains guesses, not certain information. The letter came from a person who is neutral; that person is not opposed to you."

The Duke of Cornwall said, "Cunning."

Regan added, "And false."

The Duke of Cornwall asked, "Where have you sent the King?"

"To Dover."

Regan asked, "Why to Dover? Were you not charged at peril of your life —"

The Duke of Cornwall interrupted, "Let him first tell us why he sent him to Dover."

The old Earl of Gloucester said, "I am tied to the stake, and I must stand the course. I am like a bear that has been tied to a stake and is being attacked by dogs."

Regan asked, "Why did you send King Lear to Dover?"

"Because I did not want to see your cruel fingernails pluck out his poor old eyes, nor your fierce sister stick boarish fangs in his anointed flesh.

"The sea, if it had endured such a storm as his bare head in Hell-black night, would have buoyed upward and quenched the bright lights of the stars and made the night even blacker. Yet, poor old heart, he helped the Heavens to rage and to rain by dripping his tears to the ground.

"If wolves had howled at your gate during that stern time, you would have said, 'Good porter, turn the key.' You would have ordered the gates to be opened to let the wolves in so that they could find shelter.

"During that stern time, you would not allow your poor old father to enter the gate and find shelter. Go ahead and commit all other cruel deeds, but I shall see winged vengeance overtake such children as you and your sister. Of all the evil deeds you and your sister have committed, the one that I want to see punished is your treatment of your father. The Furies punish parricides and other such sinners."

The Duke of Cornwall said, "See it you never shall."

He ordered, "Servants, hold the chair steady."

He said to the old Earl of Gloucester, "Upon these eyes of yours I'll set my foot."

The old Earl of Gloucester begged for help: "He who wants to live until he is old, give me some help! Oh, cruel man! Oh, you gods!"

The Duke of Cornwall pulled out one of the old Earl of Gloucester's eyes, dropped it on the floor, and stepped on it.

"One side of his face will mock the other side," Regan said. "Pull out the other eye, too."

The Duke of Cornwall said to the old Earl of Gloucester, "If you see vengeance —"

One of the Duke of Cornwall's servants said, "Don't move your hand, my lord. I have served you ever since I was a child, but I have never done you better service than now, when I tell you to stop."

This act took much courage on the part of the servant, and it took a strong sense of right and wrong.

Angry, Regan said, "What are you doing, you dog!"

The servant said to Regan, "If you wore a beard upon your chin, I would insult you by shaking it."

The Duke put his hand on the hilt of his sword, and the servant asked him, "What? Do you mean to fight?"

The Duke of Cornwall said, "You are my servant, and you are a villain."

The Duke of Cornwall and the servant drew swords and began to fight. The servant was a gentleman who served the Duke, and he wore a sword.

The servant wounded the Duke of Cornwall and then said, "Come on, and take the chance of fighting me while you are angry."

Regan said to another servant, "Give me your sword. I can't believe that this peasant is standing up against his master like this!"

She took the sword and ran to the servant and stabbed him in the back, inflicting a mortal wound.

The servant fell and said, "Oh, I am slain! My lord, you have one eye left to see that I have inflicted a wound on the Duke of Cornwall, who pulled out your eye."

The servant died.

The wounded Duke of Cornwall said to the old Earl of Gloucester, "Lest your remaining eye see more, I will prevent it. Out, vile jelly!"

He pulled out the remaining eye, dropped it, stepped on it, and asked, "Where is your luster now?"

The old Earl of Gloucester said, "All is dark and comfortless. Where's my son Edmund? Edmund, enkindle all the sparks of a son's love, and get revenge for this horrible act."

"Ha, treacherous villain!" Regan said. "You are calling on a person who hates you. It was Edmund who informed us about your treasons to us. Edmund is too good a person to pity you."

"I have been a fool!" the old Earl of Gloucester said. "I have wronged my son Edgar. Kind gods, forgive me for that, and help him prosper!"

Regan ordered some servants, "Go and thrust him out of the gates, and let him smell his way to Dover since he can no longer see the way."

A servant exited with the old Earl of Gloucester.

Regan asked the Duke of Cornwall, "How are you, my lord? How are you feeling, my husband?"

"I have been wounded. Come with me, lady. Turn out that eyeless villain; throw this slave — the dead servant — upon the dunghill. Regan, I am bleeding a lot. This is a bad time for me to be wounded. Give me your arm."

The Duke of Cornwall, assisted by Regan, exited.

A couple of servants remained behind.

The first servant said, "I'll never care what wickedness I do, if this man the Duke of Cornwall comes to good after he dies. I will know that no one is punished after death for the evils that they committed while they were alive."

The second servant said, "If Regan lives long, and in the end dies naturally of old age, all women will become monsters because they will know that they will not be punished for their sins."

The first servant said, "Let's go and follow the old Earl, and get the Tom o'Bedlam to lead him wherever the Earl wants to go. The Tom o'Bedlam's roguish madness allows him to do whatever he wants."

The second servant replied, "Go to the old Earl of Gloucester. I'll fetch some flax bandages and egg whites to apply to his bleeding face. Now, I pray that Heaven will help him!"

# CHAPTER 4

## — 4.1 —

The disguised Edgar was alone on the heath.

He said to himself, "It is better to be like this and know that I am despised than to be still despised and yet have people flatter me. To be the worst, the lowest, and the most rejected by Fortune means to always live in hope and not in fear. Since the worst has already happened, any change will be for the better. It is the people who are at the top of the Wheel of Fortune who will suffer a lamentable change. Welcome, then, you insubstantial air that I embrace! Let you winds blow against me! The wretch that you have blown unto the worst owes nothing to your blasts. Everything has been taken from me, and so I owe you winds of ill fortune nothing."

He saw someone coming toward him and asked himself, "But who comes here?"

An old man was leading Edgar's father, the blinded old Earl of Gloucester.

Edgar said to himself, "My father, with bloody eyes and led by a poor man? World! World! Oh, world! Except that your strange changes make us hate you, life would not accept old age. Because of the hateful changes we suffer in life, we accept old age and death."

The old man said to the old Earl of Gloucester, "Oh, my good lord, I have been your tenant, and your father's tenant, these fourscore — eighty — years."

The old Earl of Gloucester replied, "Away, get away from me, good friend. Be gone. Your comforts can do me no good at all; you may be severely punished for trying to help me."

"Alas, sir," the old man said, "you cannot see to make your way anywhere."

"I have nowhere to go, and therefore I need no eyes," the old Earl of Gloucester replied. "I stumbled when I saw. When I could see, I did not see that my legitimate son Edgar was loyal to me, and I did not see that my illegitimate son, Edmund, was disloyal to me. Very often it is seen that our possessions make us overconfident, and all of our disadvantages prove to be advantages.

"Oh, my dear son Edgar, you were the object of your deceived father's wrath! If I could only touch you again and know that you are my son, I would say I had eyes again!"

The old man saw the disguised Edgar and asked, "Hey! Who's there?"

The disguised Edgar thought, *Oh, gods! Who is it can truly say, "I am at the worst"? I just said it, but seeing my father like this makes me worse than ever I was.*

The old man looked closely and then said, "It is poor mad Tom."

The disguised Edgar thought, *And worse I may yet be: The worst has not happened as long as we can say, "This is the worst." As long as we are alive, something worse can happen to us.*

The old man asked the disguised Edgar, "Fellow, where are you going?"

The old Earl of Gloucester asked, "Is he a beggar?"

"He is a madman and a beggar, too."

"He has some reason left; otherwise, he could not beg. In last night's storm, I saw such a fellow who made me think that a man is a worm, the lowest of creatures. I remembered my son although I thought badly of him at that time. I have heard more about my son since then. As flies are to cruel boys, so are we to the gods. They torment and kill us for their entertainment."

The disguised Edgar thought, *How can this be? How did my father come to be blinded and in such circumstances that he thinks that the gods are out to torture us? But I must play Tom o'Bedlam in front of my father. Bad is the trade that must play fool to sorrow, angering itself and others. The person playing a fool resents it, as well as the sorrowful man and the bystanders.*

He said out loud, "Bless you, master!"

The old Earl of Gloucester asked the old man, "Is that the naked fellow?"

The disguised Edgar was still wearing only a blanket.

"Yes, my lord."

"Then please leave. If, for my sake, you will catch up with us, a mile or two from here, on the road toward Dover, do it out of the love and respect that you have had for me, and bring some covering for this naked soul, whom I'll entreat to lead me."

"Alas, sir, he is insane."

"It is the plague of the times, when madmen lead the blind," the old Earl of Gloucester replied. "Our leaders are insane, and they lead their blind and ignorant subjects. Do as I order you, or rather, do what you please since I cannot order anyone anymore to do anything. Most important of all, leave. You ought not to be seen with me."

The old man said, "I'll bring him the best apparel that I have, no matter what happens as a result."

The old man exited.

The old Earl of Gloucester said, "Sirrah, naked fellow —"

The disguised Edgar replied, "Poor Tom's a-cold."

He thought, *I can't do this any longer —*

"Come here, fellow."

*— and yet I must.*

The disguised Edgar said, "Bless your sweet eyes, they bleed."

"Do you know the way to Dover?"

"Both stile and gate, bridle-path and foot-path. Poor Tom has been scared out of his good wits. May the gods bless you, good man's son, and protect you from the foul fiend! Five fiends have been in poor Tom at once: Obidicut, fiend of lust; Hobbididence, fiend of dumbness; Mahu, fiend of stealing; Modo, fiend of murder; and Flibbertigibbet, fiend of grimacing and making faces, who has since possessed chambermaids and waiting-women. So, bless you, master!"

The old Earl of Gloucester said, "Here, take this wallet, you whom the Heavens' plagues have humbled so that you endure all strokes. My wretchedness makes the Heavens happy. Heavens, continue to afflict the well-off! Let the man with excess wealth who eats excess food, who treats what gods' decrees have given him as his just due, who will not see the needs of the poor because he does not feel the needs of the poor, use your power quickly — make him suffer the needs of the poor. If you do that, those who have too much shall give to those who lack enough, and each man shall have enough.

"Do you know Dover?"

The disguised Edgar replied, "Yes, master."

"At Dover is a cliff, whose high and bending head looks fearfully at the sea it overhangs and holds back. Bring me to the very brim of it, and I'll repair the misery you endure by giving you something costly that I have with me. You shall not need to lead me away from that place."

"Give me your arm. Poor Tom shall lead you."

Having finished their journey, Goneril and Edmund stood in front of the Duke of Albany's castle.

Using the royal plural, Goneril said to Edmund, "Welcome, my lord. I marvel that our mild husband did not meet us on the way."

Oswald walked up to them.

Goneril asked him, "Now, where's your master?"

Oswald replied, "Madam, he is within the castle, but I have never seen a man so changed. I told him about the French army that has landed, and he smiled. I told him that you were coming, and his answer was 'So much the worse.' I told him about the old Earl of Gloucester's treachery and about the loyal service of his son Edmund. After I informed him, he called me a fool, and he told me that I had turned the wrong side out. What he should most dislike seems pleasant to him; what he should most like seems offensive to him."

The Duke of Albany was able to see the true character of people. He knew that the old Earl of Gloucester was a good man and that the Earl's illegitimate son, Edmund, was a bad man. He also had learned and was angry about the treatment and insanity of King Lear.

Goneril said to Edmund, "Then you shall go no further. You shall not enter the castle. My husband's spirit is like a cow's; he is cowardly. He will not undertake any great endeavor. He will ignore insults that require him to retaliate. The things we talked about and hoped for on our journey may come true."

Goneril had fallen in love with Edmund.

She continued, "Go back, Edmund, to my brother-in-law; make him call up his troops quickly and then escort his armies to the place of battle. I must change arms at home, and give the woman's distaff into my husband's hands. I will be the man and wear the sword, and he shall be the woman and do the spinning and weaving. This trustworthy servant shall pass messages between us. Before long you are likely to hear, if you dare to risk action in your own behalf, a mistress' command."

She was hinting that she would ask him to kill her husband so she could be his wife.

She took off a necklace and gave it to him, saying, "Wear this; don't speak. Bow your head."

She kissed him and said, "This kiss, if it dared to speak, would raise your spirits up into the air. Conceive — understand what I mean — and fare you well."

Her words had a sexual undertone. She meant that something other than spirits would also rise into the air. This could result in the conception of a child.

Edmund, the new Earl of Gloucester, replied, "Yours in the ranks of death. I am yours until I die."

His words also had a sexual undertone. In this society, the phrase "to die" was a euphemism for "to have an orgasm."

Goneril pretended to be shocked: "My very dear Gloucester!"

Edmund exited.

Goneril said to herself, "Oh, the difference between one man and another man! Edmund, a woman's services are your due. My fool of a husband usurps my body."

Although Goneril had said that her husband would not react to insults, she had not wanted her husband to see Edmund wearing her necklace; therefore, she had sent Edmund away as soon as they arrived at her husband's castle.

Oswald said, "Madam, here comes my lord."

He exited.

The Duke of Albany, Goneril's husband, walked over to her.

Goneril said, "I have been worth the whistle."

She was alluding to the proverb "It is a poor dog that is not worth whistling for." She was saying that at one time her husband would have ridden his horse to meet her as she journeyed back to their castle.

The Duke of Albany had once loved Goneril, but he did not like the way that she had treated her father. He had not been present during King Lear's treatment at the Earl of Gloucester's castle, but he had since been informed about it.

"Oh, Goneril! You are not worth the dust that the rough and rude wind blows in your face. I fear your character. That nature, which condemns its own origins and father, cannot be trusted to stay within the bounds of morality and of good behavior. By cutting yourself away from your father, you are like a branch that has cut itself away from its tree. You, like the branch, have cut yourself off from the nourishing source and must necessarily wither and come to a bad end."

"Say no more; the text of your sermon is foolish."

"Wisdom and goodness seem vile to vile people. To filthy people, everything seems filthy. What have you done? You and your sister are tigers, not daughters. What have you done? You have made insane a father, a gracious man whose age and reverence even a captive bear enraged by being worried by dogs would lick. You are very barbarous and degenerate! Could my good brother-in-law permit you to do it? The Duke of Cornwall was a man, a Prince, whom King Lear has much benefited! If the Heavens do not quickly send down their spirits in visible form to tame these vile offenses, it will necessarily happen that Humanity prey on itself and become cannibals like monsters of the deep sea."

"You are a milk-livered man!" Goneril replied. "You are a coward! You turn your cheek so it can be hit with blows, and your head is filled with wrong ideas."

In Matthew 5:39 Jesus said, "*But I say unto you, Resist not evil: but whosoever shall smite thee on thy right cheek, turn to him the other also*" (1599 Geneva Bible). This was one "wrong idea" that Goneril had accused her husband of having.

Goneril continued, "You do not have in your brows an eye that can tell the difference between the wrong to your honor against which you must retaliate and the lesser wrong that you can endure. You do not know that only fools pity criminals who are punished before they have done their crimes. Where's your military drum? Why aren't you out raising troops? The King of France spreads his military banners in our quiet and peaceful land where no British military drums can be heard. With a plumed helmet your slayer begins to threaten you, and all you, a moralizing fool, do is to sit still, and cry, 'Oh, no, why is he acting like this?'"

"Look at yourself, Devil! Your evil shows in your appearance. Such deformity is proper for the fiend, but it is horrible in a woman."

"Oh, you vain fool!" Goneril replied.

"You have changed and that change shows in your appearance. You should be ashamed," the Duke of Albany said.

"Be-monster not your appearance," he continued. "Do not look like a monster. If it were appropriate to me to allow these hands to obey my anger, they would be ready to dislocate and tear your flesh and bones.

"Although you are a fiend, your woman's shape shields you from my anger. Continue to appear in the shape of a woman, or I will hurt you, you fiend."

"By God, you mention your manliness!" Goneril replied. "You compared to a real man are like a kitten compared to a tiger!"

A messenger arrived.

The Duke of Albany asked, "What is the news?"

"Oh, my good lord, the Duke of Cornwall's dead," the messenger replied. "He was slain by his servant as he was about to put out the other eye of the Earl of Gloucester."

"Gloucester's eye!"

"A servant that the Duke of Cornwall bred, stirred to action by pity, opposed the act, turning his sword against his great master, who, enraged by this, flew at him, and among the other people present struck him dead, but first he received that harmful stroke that a little later killed him — he followed the servant in death."

The Duke of Albany said, "This shows you are above, you Heavenly judges, who so speedily can avenge the crimes people commit on Earth! But, poor Gloucester! Did he lose his other eye?"

The messenger replied, "He lost both eyes — both, my lord."

The messenger then handed Goneril a letter and said, "This letter, madam, craves a speedy answer; it is from your sister."

Goneril thought, *In one way I like this news well. However, now that my sister Regan is a widow, and my Edmund, the new Earl of Gloucester, is with her, all the things that I have been daydreaming about — all the castles that I have built on the clouds — may crash to the ground and leave me only the hateful life I now lead. But in another way, the news is not so sour — Edmund may yet be mine and we will not have to worry about the Duke of Cornwall as a rival to our controlling all of my father's kingdom.*

She said out loud, "I'll read the letter, and answer it."

She exited.

The Duke of Albany asked the messenger, "When they blinded his eyes, where was his son Edmund?"

"He was coming here with my lady, your wife."

"He is not here."

"No, my good lord; I met him on his way back to Regan's castle again."

"Does Edmund know about this wicked act?"

"Yes, my good lord; it was he who informed against his father," the messenger said. "He left his father's castle on purpose, so that they could freely inflict their punishment on his father."

Referring to the old Earl of Gloucester, the Duke of Albany said, "Gloucester, I live so that I can thank you for the love you showed to the King, and to revenge the loss of your eyes. Come with me, friend. Tell me what else you know."

At the French camp near Dover, the disguised Kent talked to a gentleman, the same one whom he had asked to go to Dover and give a just and truthful report of how King Lear was being treated.

Kent asked, "Why has the King of France so suddenly gone back to France? Do you know the reason?"

"He left some state business unfinished, business that has become urgent since he came here; since neglecting it could put French citizens in danger and make them fearful, his personal return was required and necessary."

"Who has he left behind him as General of his army?"

"The Marshal of France, Monsieur La Far."

"Did the letter you wrote and gave to Cordelia, the Queen of France, move her to any demonstration of grief?"

"Yes, sir," the gentleman replied. "She took the letter and read it in my presence, and now and then a large tear trickled down her delicate cheek. It seemed like she was a Queen over her emotions — emotions that, most rebel-like, sought to be King over her."

"Oh, then the letter moved her," the disguised Kent said.

"She was moved, but she maintained control of her emotions. She did not allow herself to be enraged; self-control and sorrow strove to see which could make her lovelier. You have seen sunshine and rain at the same time. Her smiles and tears were like that, but better. Those happy little smiles that played on her ripe lips seemed not to know what guests — tears — were in her eyes. Her tears parted from her eyes, as if pearls were dropping from diamonds. In brief, sorrow would be a rarity most beloved, if it made everyone as lovely as Cordelia."

"Did she ask any questions or say anything?"

"Once or twice she cried with difficulty the name of 'father,' panting as if the word weighed heavily on her heart. She cried, 'Sisters! Sisters! Shame of ladies! Sisters! Kent! Father! Sisters! What, in the storm? In the night? Let pity not be believed!' There she shook the holy water from her Heavenly eyes, and she mourned without making a sound and then went away to deal with her grief alone."

The disguised Kent said, "It is the stars, the stars above us, that govern our characters; otherwise, one man and one woman could not beget daughters as different as Cordelia and her sisters. Have you spoken with her since then?"

"No."

"Was this before the King returned?"

"No, it was since the King returned."

"Well, sir, the poor distressed King Lear is in the town. Sometimes, in his better and more lucid moments, when he is less jangled and more in tune, he remembers why we are here, and he by no means will agree to see his daughter."

"Why, good sir?"

"An overbearing shame makes him remember what he would like to have never happened: his own unkindness to Cordelia that stripped from her his blessing, turned her out to find a life in a foreign land, and gave what was valuable and rightfully hers to his dog-hearted daughters. These things sting his mind so venomously that his burning shame keeps him from seeing Cordelia."

"That poor man!" the gentleman said.

"Have you heard anything about the armies of the Duke of Albany and the Duke of Cornwall?"

"Yes, they are marching toward us."

"Well, sir, I'll bring you to our master Lear, and leave you to attend him. Some important reason causes me to stay in disguise for a while. When I reveal my identity, you shall not have reason to regret being my friend. Please, come with me."

In a tent, Cordelia and a doctor were talking in the presence of some soldiers.

"Alas, my father has been seen, and he is in a bad way," Cordelia said. "Why, he was met just now. He is as mad as the vexed sea. He was singing aloud, crowned with the weed known as fumitory or earth-smoke and with the rank weeds that grow among the crops in plowed land. He wore as a crown burdocks, hemlock, nettles, cuckoo-flowers, darnel, and all the useless weeds that grow in the plowed fields along with the crops that nourish us. Send a hundred soldiers out to find him. They can search every acre in the high-grown field, and bring him before our eyes."

An officer departed to carry out the order.

She asked the doctor, "What can man's wisdom do to restore his bereaved sense? He who cures him can have all my material possessions."

"There is a way, madam," the doctor said. "The foster-nurse of Nature is sleep, which King Lear is lacking. Many herbal medicines will close his eyes of anguish and make him sleep."

"All blessed secrets, all you little-known virtuous powerful herbs of the Earth, spring up — be watered with my tears!" Cordelia cried as she prayed aloud. "Be a helpful remedy for the good man's distress."

She added, "Seek, seek for him, lest his ungoverned rage dissolve the life that lacks the means — reason — to lead it. He is likely to commit suicide because he lacks the reason needed to control himself."

A messenger entered the tent.

"I have news, madam. The British armies are marching here."

"That is something that we already knew," she replied. "Our armed troops are prepared to fight them. Oh, dear father, it is your business that I go about."

In Luke 2:49 Jesus said, "*Then said he unto them, How is it that ye sought me? Knew ye not that I must go about my Father's business?*" (1599 Geneva Bible).

Cordelia continued, "My husband, the great King of France, has pitied my mourning and importunate tears and allowed me to help my father. We are not taking up arms because of any puffed-up ambition to gain territory for ourselves, but love, dear love, makes us fight for our aged father's rights. I hope that soon I may hear and see him!"

Regan and Oswald, Goneril's steward, were talking together in the castle of the Earl of Gloucester.

Regan asked, "Have the armies of my brother-in-law, the Duke of Albany, set forth?

"Yes, madam."

"Is the Duke of Albany, himself, leading them in person?"

"Yes, madam, but it took much persuading. Your sister is the better soldier."

The Duke of Albany had thought hard about where his loyalties should lie: Should he fight for Cordelia and King Lear, or should he resist the armies of France?

"Did Lord Edmund speak with your lord, the Duke of Albany, at home?"

"No, madam."

"My sister has written a letter to Edmund. What does she write in that letter?"

Regan was jealous. She wanted Edmund.

"I don't know, lady."

"Truly, Edmund rode away in a hurry on important business," Regan said. "It was political folly to allow the old Earl of Gloucester to remain alive after we put out his eyes. Wherever he goes, he moves all hearts against us. They pity him, and hate us. Edmund, I think, has gone, out of pity for his father's misery, to kill him and end his benighted life. Also, he left in order to determine the strength of the enemy."

"I must go after him, madam, with my lady's letter," Oswald said.

"Our troops set forth tomorrow. Stay and travel with us. The roads are dangerous."

"I may not do so, madam. My lady was very insistent that I do my duty and deliver this letter."

"Why should she write to Edmund? Why couldn't you have simply communicated verbally her message to him? Perhaps, she wanted to say ... I don't know what. I'll greatly appreciate it if you will let me unseal the letter and read it."

"Madam, I had rather —"

Regan said, "I know your lady, Goneril, does not love her husband. I am sure of that. When she was here recently, she looked at noble Edmund strangely and admiringly and very meaningfully. I know that she confides in you — you are close to her bosom."

"I, madam?"

"I know what I know," Regan said. "You are; I know it. Therefore, I advise you, take careful note of what I now say to you. My lord and husband is dead; Edmund and I have talked and reached an understanding. It is more convenient and suitable for him to marry me than to marry your lady. From what I have said, you may guess the rest. If you find Edmund, please give him this ring. And when you tell your mistress all that has happened here, tell her to come to her senses — I and not she will have Edmund. So, fare you well. If you happen to hear of that blind traitor Gloucester, know that whoever kills him will be rewarded."

Oswald said, "I wish that I could meet him, madam! I would show whose side I am on!"

"Fare you well."

In a field near Dover, Edgar, who was now dressed like a peasant, was leading his blinded father, the old Earl of Gloucester, who wanted to be taken to a cliff near Dover so that he could commit suicide. Edgar, however, did not want his father to die, and he had not led him to the cliff.

The old Earl of Gloucester asked, "When shall we come to the top of the hill at Dover?"

"You are climbing up it now," Edgar lied. "See how hard it is to climb this hill."

"I think that the ground is even."

"It is horribly steep. Listen, do you hear the sea?"

"No, truly I don't."

"Why, then, your other senses grow imperfect now that your eyes are blind."

"That may be true, indeed," the old Earl of Gloucester said. "I think that your voice has changed and that you speak more articulately and with better content than you did."

"You're much deceived," the disguised Edgar lied. "I am changed in nothing except that I am wearing different clothing."

"I think that you are better spoken now."

"Come on, sir; here's the place," the disguised Edgar said. "Stand still. How dreadful and dizzy it is to cast one's eyes so low! The crows and jackdaws that wing the midway air seem scarcely as large as beetles. Halfway down the cliff hangs a man gathering samphire, an herb used in pickling — his is a dreadful line of work! I think that from here he seems to be no bigger than his head. The fishermen, whom I see walking upon the beach, appear to be the size of mice; and yonder I see a tall ship at anchor that seems to be the size of its small rowboat; the small rowboat itself seems to be the size of a buoy — it is almost too small to be seen from here. The murmuring waves that chafe innumerable useless pebbles cannot be heard so high. I'll look no more lest my brain grow giddy, and my deficient sight cause me to topple headlong from the cliff!"

The old Earl of Gloucester said, "Set me where you are standing."

"Give me your hand," the disguised Edgar said, moving his father into position. "You are now within a foot of the edge. I would not jump up and down for all that lies beneath the Moon because of fear of falling."

"Let go of my hand. Here, friend, is another wallet; in it is a jewel well worth a poor man's taking. May fairies and gods help you to prosper with it! Go farther away, tell me farewell, and let me hear you going."

"Now fare you well, good sir."

"With all my heart."

The disguised Edgar thought, *I seem to be trifling with my father's despair, but I am doing this to cure it. My father now thinks that the gods are like cruel boys who tear the wings off flies; he thinks that the gods torment and kill us for their entertainment.*

The old Earl of Gloucester knelt and prayed, "Oh, you mighty gods! This world I renounce, and, in your sights, I shake off my great affliction patiently. If I could bear my great affliction longer, and not fall and quarrel with your great wills that cannot be opposed, my last remaining and loathed part of life should burn itself out naturally. If Edgar is still alive, gods, bless him!"

He then said to the disguised Edgar, who was far enough away not to stop him from jumping, "Now, fellow, fare you well."

He fell forward. He was not at the cliffs of Dover, so he did not die.

The disguised Edgar said out loud, "Gone, sir. Farewell."

He thought, *And yet, although I do not know how, imagination may rob the treasure of life, when life itself consents to the theft. He may be dead simply because he wants to be dead, although he did not fall from a great height. Had he been where he thought he was, on the cliffs of Dover, he would have been past thought by this time — he would be dead. Is he alive or is he dead?*

Edgar changed his voice and said, "Ho, you sir! Friend! Can you hear me, sir! Speak!"

He thought, *My father might very well be dead indeed, yet he revives.*

He asked out loud, "Who are you, sir?"

His father said, "Go away, and let me die."

The disguised Edgar said, "Had you been anything but gossamer, feathers, air, falling precipitously so many fathoms down, you would have smashed into pieces like an egg, but you are breathing, have a heavy body, are not bleeding, speak, and are sound and healthy. Ten masts stacked vertically end to end would not reach the altitude from which you have perpendicularly fallen. Your being alive is a miracle. Speak once more."

"But have I fallen, or not?"

"You fell from the dread summit of this chalky cliff that forms a boundary of the sea. Look up at the height; the shrill-voiced lark cannot be seen or heard so far from here. Look up."

"I grieve because I have no eyes. Is wretchedness deprived of that benefit: to end itself by suicide? It was yet some comfort when a miserable man could cheat the tyrant's rage and frustrate his proud will by committing suicide rather than bending to his will."

"Give me your arm. Let me help you up. Good. How are you? Can you feel your legs? You are standing."

"Too well, too well," the old Earl of Gloucester said.

"This is the strangest thing that I have ever seen. Upon the crown of the cliff, what thing was that which parted from you?"

"A poor unfortunate beggar."

"As I stood here below, I thought his eyes were two full Moons; he had a thousand noses, his horns were curved and waved like the furrowed sea. It was some fiend; therefore, you fortunate old man, think that the gods who are most clearly known by men to be gods, who get honor for themselves by performing miracles that are impossible for men to perform, have preserved you and saved your life with a miracle."

In this society, people who committed suicide were thought to end up in Hell. Demons were thought to tempt discouraged men to commit suicide so that they would be eternally damned.

"I remember the correct way to think about the gods now; henceforth, I'll bear affliction until it itself cries, 'Enough, enough,' and then I will die. That thing you speak of, I took it for a man; often it would say, 'The fiend, the fiend.' He led me to that place."

"Think correctly. Do not engage in self-despair. Be patient and engage in self-control," the disguised Edgar said. "But I see someone coming here. Who is it?"

King Lear, still insane, was dressed in odd, fantastic clothing, and he was wearing a crown of weeds.

The disguised Edgar thought, *No one in his right mind would dress like that and wear a crown like that.*

King Lear said, "No, they cannot arrest me for counterfeiting coins; I am the King himself and I have the right to coin money."

"What a pitiful and heart-rending sight!" the disguised Edgar said.

"Nature's above art in that respect," King Lear said. "You can see more pitiful and heart-rending sights in real life than you do in art."

Thinking about money made King Lear think about soldiers and paying them.

To an imaginary soldier, he said, "There's your money for being impressed into the army."

About another imaginary soldier, he said, "That fellow handles his bow like a scarecrow. Draw the arrow back as far as it will go."

Military combat on a grand scale made him think of another combat on a small scale: "Look, look, a mouse! Peace, peace; this piece of toasted cheese will tempt the mouse so that I can kill it."

Combat with a mouse made him think of a grander combat: "There's my gauntlet; I have thrown it on the ground as a challenge. I'll defend my case and prove myself in the right even if I have to defeat a giant."

He thought about other kinds of soldiers: those who carried pikes and those who were archers: "Bring up the brown bills — those who carry pikes painted brown to prevent rust. Oh, well flown, bird and arrow! In the bull's-eye! In the bull's-eye! Thud!"

Seeing Edgar, he said, "Give me the password."

The disguised Edgar replied, "Sweet marjoram."

This was an herb used to treat insanity.

"Correct!" King Lear said.

The old Earl of Gloucester said, "I recognize that voice."

Seeing Gloucester's white beard, King Lear thought that he was seeing one of his daughters in disguise: "Ha! Goneril, wearing a white beard! They flattered me as if they were fawning dogs, and they told me I had white hairs in my beard before the black ones were there — they said I was wise even before I grew a beard. They said 'yes' and 'no' to everything that I said 'yes' and 'no' to — this was bad theology."

These verses are II Corinthians 18-19 (King James Version):

King Lear remembered the storm that he had endured: "When the rain came to wet me on one occasion, and the wind came to make my teeth chatter; when the thunder would not stop at my order; there I discovered that these people were flatterers — I smelled them out. Believe me, they are not men of their words: they told me I was everything and all-powerful; it is a lie, for I am not fever-proof."

"I well remember that distinctive voice," the old Earl of Gloucester said. "Isn't it the King?"

King Lear replied, "Yes, I am every inch a King. When I stare at a subject, see how the subject quakes."

Looking at the old Earl of Gloucester, he said, "I pardon that man's life. What was your crime? Adultery? You shall not die. Die for adultery! No. The wren goes to it and fornicates, and the small gilded fly fornicates in my sight. Let copulation thrive. Why? Because Gloucester's bastard son, Edmund, was kinder to his father than my daughters have been to me even though I fathered my daughters between lawful sheets with my properly married wife. Go to it, lechery, go to it hot and heavy! I lack soldiers, and fornication will bring me many soldiers."

King Lear then stated his current opinion of women: "Behold yonder simpering dame, whose face between her hair-combs seems to be a sign of snowy chastity and who seems to be fastidiously virtuous. She shakes her head if she merely hears the name of pleasure, but neither the polecat-like whores, nor the frisky and lecherous horses go at it with a more riotous appetite. Down from the waist women are lustful Centaurs, although they are women all above the waist. What is above the waist belongs to the gods, but what is beneath belongs to the foul fiends. There's Hell, there's darkness, there's the sulfurous pit, burning, scalding, stench, consumption. Wham! Bam!"

Hell was a word sometimes used in this culture to refer to the vagina.

King Lear then spoke to the old Earl of Gloucester as if the Earl were a pharmacist: "Give me an ounce of perfume, good apothecary, to sweeten my imagination. Here's some money for you."

The old Earl of Gloucester said, "Oh, let me kiss that hand!"

King Lear replied, "Let me wipe it first; it smells of death and human mortals."

The old Earl of Gloucester said, referring to King Lear, "Oh, ruined piece of human nature! This great world shall likewise wear out to nothing. Do you know me?"

King Lear replied, "I remember your eyes well enough. Are you squinting at me? No, do your worst, blind Cupid! I'll not love."

In this society, brothels used a depiction of a blind Cupid as their sign.

King Lear said, holding an imaginary document, "Read this challenge; see the way that it is written."

"Even if all the letters were Suns, I could not see even one."

The disguised Edgar thought, *I would not believe this if someone told me this, but it is real, and my heart breaks because of it.*

King Lear said, "Read this document."

The old Earl of Gloucester replied, "How? With my eye sockets?"

King Lear said, "Oh, ho, are you there with me? Are we similar? Are we both blind? No eyes in your head, and no money in your wallet? Your eyes are in a heavy and serious situation because your eye sockets are empty. Your wallet is in a light and serious situation because it is empty. Yet you can still see how this world goes."

"I see the world feelingly. I see the world keenly through my sense of touch."

King Lear replied, "What, are you insane? A man with no eyes may see how this world goes. Look with your ears. See yonder how a judge scolds a common thief. Pay attention with your ears. Let the judge and the common thief change places, and — make a guess — which is the justice and which is the thief? Have you seen a farmer's dog bark at a beggar?"

The old Earl of Gloucester replied, "Yes, sir."

"And have you seen the creature run away from the cur?" King Lear asked. "There you can behold the great image of authority: a dog is obeyed when it is in office."

Imagining that he saw a parish constable punishing a prostitute by whipping her, King Lear said, "You rascal constable, hold your bloody hand! Why do you lash that whore? Strip your own back and stripe it with lashes. You hotly lust to use her in that kind of sin for which you are whipping her."

He then said, "The usurer hangs the cozener. The big thief hangs the small thief. Through tattered clothes small vices can be seen; the robes and furred gowns of the great hide all their sins. Cover the sinner with gold-plated armor, and the strong lance of justice breaks against it without causing hurt to the sinner. But if the sinner's armor consists of rags, a pigmy's straw is able to pierce it.

"No one offends and commits sins — no one, I say, no one. I'll vouch for them and give them immunity from prosecution. Take it from me, my friend — I have the power to close the accuser's lips. Get yourself glass eyes, and then, like a scurvy schemer, pretend that you see the things you do not."

He then said to the old Earl of Gloucester as if he were his valet: "Now, now, now, now. Pull off my boots. Pull harder, harder. Good."

The disguised Edgar said, "Oh, the King's speech is a mixture of sense and nonsense! Reason in the midst of madness!"

King Lear said to the old Earl of Gloucester, "If you will weep over my fortunes, take my eyes. I know you well enough; your name is Gloucester. You must be patient and have self-control; we came crying hither. You know that the first time that we smell and breathe the air — when we are born — we wail and cry. I will preach to you. Listen."

"This is too sad," the old Earl of Gloucester said.

King Lear stood on a stump and said, "When we are born, we cry because we have come to this great stage of fools. This stump is a good mounting-block to stand on to mount a horse. It is a neat stratagem to shoe military horses with felt to deaden the noise their hooves make. I'll give it a try, and when I have stolen upon these sons-in-law of mine, then kill, kill, kill, kill, kill, kill! No quarter!"

A gentleman arrived, accompanied by some attendants.

He said, "Oh, here he is. Lay your hands upon him."

He said to King Lear, "Sir, your most dear daughter —"

King Lear, who had just thought about attacking his sons-in-law, now thought that he had been captured. He said, "No rescue? What, am I a prisoner? I was born to be the plaything of Fortune. Treat me well; I am a King, and you shall receive much ransom for me. Let me have surgeons to treat my injury; I am cut to the brains."

King Lear's brains were vexed; the physical head wound he thought that he had received was imaginary.

The gentleman said, "You shall have anything you need."

"No supporters? I am all by myself?" King Lear said. "Why, this would make a man a man of salt tears — he could use his eyes for watering pots to tend the garden and to wet the streets so that the dust of autumn would not rise in the air."

The gentleman said to King Lear, "Good sir —"

"I will die bravely, like a bridegroom," King Lear said. "What! I will be jovial."

He was punning. One meaning of "die" was "to have an orgasm." "Bravely" could mean "courageously" or "finely dressed."

He added, "I am a King, my masters; you need to know that."

"You are a royal one, and we obey you," the gentleman said.

"Then there is still hope," King Lear said. "If you get your prize — take me captive — you shall get it with running."

He ran away. As he did so, he cried, "Sa! Sa! Sa! Sa!"

These were words used by hunters to encourage their dogs to track their prey.

The attendants of the gentleman ran after him, but the gentleman stayed with the disguised Edgar and the old Earl of Gloucester.

The gentleman said, "This sight would be extremely pitiful if the meanest wretch were acting this way, but to see a King acting this way is past speaking of! You, King Lear, have one daughter who redeems human nature from the universal curse that two — Goneril and Regan, and maybe even Adam and Eve — have brought her to."

"Hello, gentle sir," the disguised Edgar said.

"Sir, may God make you prosper," the gentleman replied. "What do you want?"

"Have you heard anything, sir, of an upcoming battle?"

"The battle, as is commonly known, will surely take place. Everyone who can understand sound and words has heard that."

"Please tell me how near the other army is."

"It is near and marching quickly. We think that the main part of the army will arrive any hour now."

"I thank you, sir. That's all I have to ask you."

"Although Cordelia, the Queen of France, is here for a special reason, her army has moved on."

"I thank you, sir."

The gentleman departed.

The old Earl of Gloucester said, "You ever-gentle gods, take my breath away from me. Let not my worse spirit, aka bad angel, tempt me again to die — by suicide! — before you gods please!"

The old Earl of Gloucester still wanted to die, but he did not want to commit suicide.

"That is a good prayer, father," the disguised Edgar said.

In this society, "father" could mean "biological father," or it could simply mean "old man." Edgar had not yet revealed his identity to his father, so he was using the word "father" to mean "old man."

"Now, good sir, who are you?" the old Earl of Gloucester asked.

"I am a very poor man, made submissive by Fortune's blows. Because I have both known and felt sorrows, I am capable of feeling pity. Give me your hand, and I'll lead you to some resting place."

"I give hearty thanks to you. May you receive the bounty and the blessing of Heaven in addition to my thanks."

Oswald arrived. Seeing the old Earl of Gloucester, he said, "There is a bounty on his head that has been proclaimed throughout the land! This is very fortunate for me!"

He said to the old Earl of Gloucester, "That eyeless head of yours was first made flesh in order to raise my fortunes and make money for me. You old unhappy traitor, briefly remember your sins and pray for forgiveness. The sword that must destroy you is out of its scabbard."

The old Earl of Gloucester replied, "Now let your friendly hand put strength enough in the thrust of your sword to accomplish your goal."

Because he wanted to die, he called Oswald's hand friendly.

The disguised Edgar stood in between his father and Oswald.

"Why, bold peasant," Oswald asked, "do you dare to support a man who has been proclaimed to be a traitor? Get out of here lest the infection of his fortune take a similar hold on you. Let go of his arm."

Edgar was disguised as a peasant, and so Oswald was not afraid of him because peasants were unlikely to know how to fight against a man who was trained in swordsmanship. In addition, peasants did not carry swords. The disguised Edgar was armed with a cudgel.

Oswald had called him a peasant, and so the disguised Edgar adopted a peasant's rustic language.

"Ch'ill not let go, zir, without vurther 'casion."

["I will not go, sir, without further reason."]

"Let go of his arm, slave, or you die!" Oswald shouted.

"Good gentleman, go your gait, and let poor volk pass. An chud ha' bin zwaggered out of my life, 'twould not ha' bin zo long as it is by a vortnight. Nay, come not near th' old man. Keep out, che vor ye, or ise try whether your costard or my ballow be the harder. Ch'ill be plain with you."

["Good gentleman, go on your way, and let poor folk pass. If I could have been bullied out of my life, I would not have lived as long as I have by a fortnight. No, do not come near the old man. Keep away, or, I promise you, I will find out whether your head or my cudgel is harder. I am telling you the plain truth."]

Oswald shouted, "Go away, you dunghill!"

"Ch'ill pick your teeth, zir. Come; no matter vor your foins."

["I'll use your sword to pick your teeth, sir. Come on and fight; I am not afraid of your fencing thrusts."]

They fought, and the disguised Edgar gave Oswald a mortal wound.

Oswald fell. Dying, he said, "Slave, you have slain me. Villain, take my wallet and money. If you want to thrive, bury my body and give the letter that you will find on me to Edmund, the Earl of Gloucester. Seek him. He is on the British side. Oh, untimely and early death!"

He died.

The disguised Edgar said, "I know you well. You are a villain who helps your mistress do evil deeds; you are as duteous to the vices of your mistress as badness would desire."

"What, is he dead?" the old Earl of Gloucester said.

"Sit down, old man, and rest. Let's see what's in this fellow's pockets. The letter that he spoke about may have useful information. He's dead; I am only sorry that he had no other executioner than myself. Let us see. I beg your pardon, gentle wax that seals this letter. Manners and etiquette, do not blame us. To know our enemies' minds, we would rip their hearts; to rip their letters open is more lawful."

He read the letter out loud: "*Remember the vows we made to each other. In the battle, you will have many opportunities to cut down his life; if your will is not lacking, the time and place for committing murder will be plentifully offered. If he returns as the conqueror of the battle, then I am his prisoner, and his bed is my jail; from the loathed warmth of his bed deliver me, and in return for your labor take his place in my bed. Your — I would like to say wife, but I have to say for now — affectionate servant, GONERIL.*"

The disguised Edgar said to himself, "Oh, how vast and without limits is the lust of a woman! This is a plot upon her virtuous husband's life; she wanted to exchange her virtuous husband for Edmund, my illegitimate half-brother!"

He said to Oswald's corpse, "Here, in the sands, I'll bury you, the unholy messenger of murderous lechers, and at the right time I will show this ungracious letter to the Duke of Albany, whose death his wife plotted. For him it is a good thing that I can tell him about your death and the errand you were running."

The old Earl of Gloucester said, "The King is insane. How obstinate is my vile sense that remains sane and will not allow me to escape from my sorrows by lapsing into madness. Instead, I stand up, and I have conscious feeling of my huge sorrows! It would be better if I were insane. That way, my thoughts would be severed and divorced from my griefs, and my woes would lose the knowledge of themselves because I would see delusions."

"Give me your hand," the disguised Edgar said.

Military drums sounded.

He said, "From far away, I think, I hear the beaten drum. Come, father, I'll leave you with a friend."

In a tent in the French camp were Cordelia, the disguised Kent, the gentleman, and a doctor. Some servants were also present. Music was playing softly.

Cordelia said, "Oh, Kent, you good man, how shall I live and work to match your goodness? My life will be too short, and everything I do to try to match your goodness will fail. How can I ever repay you?"

"For you to thank me, madam, is more than enough reward. Everything that I have reported is the modest truth — no more or less, but just the truth."

"Put on a better suit of clothing," Cordelia requested. "These clothes you are wearing are reminders of those very bad hours you have told me about. Please, take them off and put on better clothing."

"Pardon me, dear madam," the disguised Kent said, "to be recognized by others now would harm the plan that I have formed. I ask for a boon from you: Pretend in public that you do not know me until I think that the time is right."

Kent's plan may have been to reveal his identity to King Lear at a time when the King would recognize him.

"Then so be it, my good lord," Cordelia replied.

She said to the doctor, "How is the King doing?"

"Madam, he is still sleeping."

Cordelia prayed, "Oh, you kind gods, cure this great illness in his abused human nature! His senses are untuned and jarring; tune them and make them harmonious. Make this man sane, this man who has been harmed by his children and who has turned back into a child in his dotage."

The doctor said, "If it pleases your majesty, we will wake the King. He has slept for a long time."

"Be governed by your knowledge, and proceed as you think best," Cordelia said. "Is he dressed?"

The gentleman said, "Yes, he is, Madam. While he was deeply asleep, we put fresh, clean garments on him."

The doctor said to Cordelia, "Be close by, good madam, when we awake him. I am sure that he will be sane."

"Very well," she replied.

Some attendants carried in King Lear.

The doctor said to the attendant, "Please, bring him close."

The doctor then ordered, "Play the music louder!" He wanted the music to wake up King Lear.

Cordelia said, "Oh, my dear father! May the god of restoration hang your medicine on my lips; and let this kiss repair those violent harms that my two sisters have made against your reverence!"

She kissed him.

The disguised Kent said, "Kind and dear Princess!"

Cordelia said to the sleeping King Lear, "Even if you had not been their father, these white strands of hair should have made Goneril and Regan pity you. Was this a face to be out in the storm and opposed against the warring winds? Was this a face to stand against the loud and dreadful thunderbolt? Was this a face to be amidst the most terrible and nimble strokes of quick, zigzag lightning? Was this a face to be in bad weather like a guard at a dangerous post — when the face had only a few strands of hair as a helmet? My enemy's dog, even if it had bitten me, would have stood that night near my fireplace — were you forced, poor father, to shelter yourself with swine, and forlorn rogues, on broken and musty straw? Alas! Alas! It is a wonder that your life and wits did not end immediately."

She said to the doctor, "He is awakening. Speak to him."

The musicians now played softly.

"Madam, you should be the one to first speak to him; it is fittest."

Cordelia said to her father, "How is my royal lord? How fares your majesty?"

King Lear said, "You do me wrong to take me out of my grave. You are a soul in bliss in Heaven, but I am bound upon a Wheel of Fire and my own tears scald me as if they were molten lead."

"Sir, do you know me?" Cordelia asked.

"You are a spirit, I know. When did you die?"

Mourning, Cordelia said to the doctor, "His wits are still far wide of the mark."

"He is barely awake," the doctor said. "Let him alone for awhile."

King Lear asked, "Where have I been? Where am I? Is this beautiful daylight and not Hell? I am mightily confused. I would die of pity if I were to see someone as confused as I am. I don't know what to say. I will not swear these are my hands. Let's see if they are."

He took the pin of a brooch and stuck one of his fingers with it.

He said, "I feel this pinprick. I wish I could be assured that I am all right and not in Hell!"

Cordelia knelt and said, "Oh, look upon me, sir, and hold your hands in benediction over me. No, sir, you must not kneel."

"Please, do not mock me," King Lear said. "I am a very foolish and senile old man. My age is fourscore and upward, not an hour more or less, and, to speak plainly, I fear that I am not in my right mind. I think that I should know who you are, and I should know who this man is."

He motioned toward the disguised Kent.

He continued, "Yet I am doubtful because I am entirely ignorant what place this is; and using all the skill and knowledge I have, I cannot remember these garments I am wearing, nor do I know where I lodged last night. Do not laugh at me. As I am a man, I think this lady is my child Cordelia."

"And so I am, I am," Cordelia said, crying because she was happy that her father recognized her.

King Lear said, "Are your tears wet? Yes, truly they are. Please, do not cry. If you have poison for me, I will drink it. I know that you do not love me because your sisters have, I remember, done me wrong. You have some reason to hate me; they have not."

"I have no reason to hate you — no reason," Cordelia said.

"Am I in France?" King Lear asked.

He remembered that Cordelia was the Queen of France.

The disguised Kent said, "You are in your own Kingdom, sir."

"Do not make fun of me," King Lear said.

He remembered that he had given his Kingdom away.

The doctor said to Cordelia, "Be comforted, good madam. The great rage of madness, you see, is killed in him, and yet it is dangerous to make him try to remember the time that he has lost due to madness. Ask him to go into his own tent; trouble him no more until after he has had more time for his mind to settle and be calm."

"Will it please your Highness to walk to your tent?" Cordelia asked her father.

"You must be patient with me," King Lear replied. "Please, forget and forgive. I am old and foolish."

Everyone left the tent except the disguised Kent and the gentleman.

The gentleman asked, "Do people still believe, sir, that the Duke of Cornwall was slain in the way that we have heard?"

"Most certainly, sir."

"Who is the general of his army?"

"We have heard that it is Edmund, the bastard son of the Earl of Gloucester."

"They say that Edgar, his banished son, is with the Earl of Kent in Germany."

The gentleman had been in the tent when the disguised Kent had revealed his identity to Cordelia. He knew who Kent was; he was simply making a point about rumors. The gentleman found it difficult to believe that the Duke of Cornwall had died as reported and that Edmund was leading the Duke's forces.

"Rumors change," the disguised Kent said, acknowledging the gentleman's point.

Then he said, "It is time to take action; the armies of the British Kingdom approach quickly."

"The final outcome is likely to be bloody. Fare you well, sir," the gentleman said as he exited.

The disguised Kent said, "My point and period will be thoroughly wrought, either well or ill, as this day's battle is fought."

He meant that the end of his life would be either good or bad, depending on how the battle ended.

# CHAPTER 5

## — 5.1 —

In the British camp, near Dover, Edmund and Regan were talking. Also present were some gentlemen and some soldiers.

Edmund said to a gentleman, "Find out from the Duke of Albany if he is still planning to follow his most recent plan — to fight against King Lear's forces — or whether he has been induced by anything to change his course of action. He is full of indecision and self-reproach. Bring me his final decision."

The gentleman left to carry out the action.

Regan said, "Oswald, the courtier of Goneril, my sister, has certainly met with misfortune."

Edmund replied, "I fear that is correct, madam."

"Now, sweet lord, you know the good things that I am planning for you. Tell me — and speak the truth. Don't you love my sister?"

"With an honorable love."

"But have you ever found my brother-in-law's way to the forbidden place? Have you ever slept with her?"

"That thought is not worthy of you."

"I am afraid that you have been joined bosom to bosom with her, in the most intimate way."

"No, by my honor, madam," Edmund said.

"I can't stand her," Regan said. "My dear lord, do not be friendly with her."

"Trust me." He heard a sound, looked up, and said, "Here she comes with the Duke of Albany, her husband."

The Duke of Albany, Goneril, and some soldiers walked over to them.

Goneril thought, *I had rather lose the battle than endure my sister coming in between Edmund and me.*

The Duke of Albany said, "Regan, our very loving sister-in-law, we are well met. Edmund, sir, I hear that King Lear has come to Cordelia, his daughter, with others whom the tyranny of our government has forced to cry out and rebel. I have never fought for a cause in which I did not believe. As for this business, it concerns me because it is an invasion of my country. I will fight for that reason, but not because the invasion emboldens the King and others who, I fear, oppose us for very just and serious reasons."

"Sir, you speak nobly," Edmund replied.

Regan asked, "Why are you telling us these reasons?"

Goneril said, "Let us join together against the enemy; these personal and private squabbles are not the issue here."

The Duke of Albany said, "Let's decide with the Chief of Staff how to proceed."

"I shall attend you immediately at your tent," Edmund said.

The Duke of Albany, Edmund, and the Chief of Staff would meet in a council of war.

Regan started to leave, but she noticed Goneril staying behind and suspected that she was planning to attend the council of war and be with Edmund.

Regan asked Goneril, "Sister, will you come with us?"

"No."

"It is very convenient; please, come with us."

Goneril thought, *I see what you want — you want to keep me away from Edmund.*

She said, "I will go with you."

Edgar, still disguised as a peasant, arrived as everyone was leaving. He said to the Duke of Albany, "If your grace has ever had speech with a man as poor as I am, listen briefly to what I have to say."

The Duke of Albany said to the others, "Go ahead of me. I will be with you soon."

He said to the disguised Edgar, "Speak."

Edgar gave him a letter — the letter that he had taken from the pocket of the dead Oswald. This was the letter in which Goneril, the Duke of Albany's wife, urged Edmund to kill her husband so that they could be married.

The disguised Edgar said, "Before you fight the battle, open this letter and read it. If you win the battle, let the trumpet sound for the man — me — who brought it. Wretched though I seem to be, I can produce a champion who will prove in a trial by combat what is avouched there. If you lose the battle, your business in the world will come to an end, and plots won't matter to you. May the goddess Fortune love you."

"Stay here until I have read the letter," the Duke of Albany requested.

"I was forbidden to stay. When time shall serve, let the herald cry and the trumpet blow, and I'll appear again."

"Why, fare you well. I will look over the letter you have brought to me."

The disguised Edgar left, and Edmund appeared.

Edmund said to the Duke of Albany, "The enemy's in view; draw up your armies."

He gave the Duke of Albany a paper and said, "Here is the estimate of the enemy's true strength and forces by our diligent scouts. Now, haste is needed."

"We will greet the time," the Duke of Albany said. "We are prepared."

He exited.

Now alone, Edmund said to himself, "To both these sisters — Goneril and Regan — I have sworn my love. Each is suspicious of the other, as those who have been bitten are suspicious of the adder. Which of them shall I take? Both? One? Or neither? Neither can be enjoyed, if both remain alive. If I were to take the widow, Regan, her sister Goneril would be exasperated and mad, and I cannot achieve my ambition if Goneril's husband, the Duke of Albany, remains alive.

"Right now we'll use him to fight for our side in the battle. After the battle, let her who would be rid of him — Goneril, who wants to marry me, or Regan, who wants to be Queen of all Britain — devise his speedy death. As for the mercy that he intends to show to Lear and to Cordelia, once the battle is done, and they are within our power, they shall never see his pardon. My situation requires that I take action, not engage in debate about how to treat the royal prisoners."

For Edmund to become King of Britain, several people would have to die: King Lear, Cordelia, the Duke of Albany, and either Goneril or Regan. He would marry the surviving sister.

Edgar led his father, the blinded old Earl of Gloucester, to a tree and said, "Here, father, take the shadow of this tree as your good host; pray that the right side may thrive. If I ever return to you again, I'll bring you comfort."

He still had not told his father his real identity; he planned to do that after the battle, if he survived.

"May grace go with you, sir!"

Edgar left.

The battle was fought, and trumpets called for retreat.

Edgar came back to his father and said, "We need to get away, old man; give me your hand. We need to get away! King Lear has lost the battle; he and his daughter have been captured. Give me your hand; come on."

"No farther, sir; a man may rot even here."

"What, are you in ill thoughts again? Men must endure their going hence, even as they endured their coming hither. We are born, and we must die. Ripeness is all; it is everything. An apple grows ripe and falls from the tree and dies. The gods decide when a death is ripe; we do not. We must endure, and we must not commit suicide. We must take death when the gods give it to us."

The old Earl of Gloucester said, "That's true."

In the British camp, Edmund stood with King Lear and Cordelia as his prisoners. Also present were a captain and some soldiers, some of whom were guarding King Lear and Cordelia.

Edmund ordered, "Some officers take the prisoners away under good guard until we know what the higher-ups who are to judge the prisoners tell us what to do."

Cordelia said to King Lear, "We are not the first who, with the best intentions, have suffered the worst. The goddess Fortune has cast me down because I wanted to help you, oppressed King, my father. I am sorry that I could not help you, father; otherwise, I would out-frown false Fortune's frown."

She then asked Edmund, "Shall we not see these daughters and these sisters?"

King Lear said, "No! No! No! No! Come, let's go away to prison. We two alone will sing like birds in the cage. When you ask me for my blessing, I'll kneel down and ask you to forgive me. In this way we'll live, and pray, and sing, and tell old tales, and laugh at gilded butterflies and hear poor rogues — fancily dressed courtiers and such other people — talk about court news; and we'll talk with them, too, about who loses and who wins, and who's in and who's out of the King's favor. We will act as if we are God's spies and can understand the mystery of things, and we'll wear out, in a walled prison, packs and sects of great ones, who ebb and flow by the moon. They will come and go, but we will be together."

Edmund ordered, "Take them away."

King Lear said, "Upon such sacrifices as our renunciation of the world, my Cordelia, the gods themselves throw incense — they approve. Have I caught you? Are you really here with me? He who parts us shall bring a brand from Heaven, and use fire and smoke to drive us out of jail like they drive foxes out of kennels. Since no one is able to bring a brand from Heaven, we will stay together. Heaven will not assist them in separating us again. Wipe your eyes. The devils shall devour our enemies, flesh and skin together, before they shall make us weep. We'll see them starve first. Come with me."

King Lear and Cordelia left, heavily guarded.

Edmund said, "Come here, captain, and listen to me."

He gave the captain a note and said, "Take this note, and go and follow them to prison. One step I have already promoted you; if you do as this note instructs you to do, then you will have made your way to noble fortunes. You should know that men are as the times are: When times are hard, men are hard. To be tender-minded does not become a soldier. This task I want you to do will not bear discussion — you are not to question it. Either say you will do it, or find another way to thrive."

"I'll do it, my lord."

"Go about it and know that you will be a happy man when you have finished. Remember, I say, to follow your instructions immediately, and follow your instructions exactly as I have written them."

The captain said, "I am not a horse. I cannot draw a cart, nor eat dried oats. If it is man's work, I'll do it."

He left.

The Duke of Albany, Goneril, Regan, a different captain, and some soldiers arrived.

Using the royal plural, the Duke of Albany said to Edmund, "Sir, you have shown today your valiant lineage and disposition, and the goddess Fortune led you well. You have the captives who were our enemies during this day's strife. We command you to hand them over to us so that we can treat them as we shall find that their merits and our safety may equally determine."

Playing for time in which the captain could accomplish his task, Edmund replied, "Sir, I thought it fit to send the old and miserable King Lear to some confinement under appointed guard. The King's age has charms in it, and his title has more charms, that will make the common people take his side and make the lance-equipped soldiers we drafted to turn against us who command them. With him I sent Cordelia, the Queen of France, for the same reason. They are ready tomorrow, or at a further time, to appear wherever you shall hold your session and judge them. At this time we sweat and bleed. In the battle, the friend has lost his friend. And the best causes, in the heat of battle, are cursed by those who feel their sharpness. The question of Cordelia and her father requires a fitter place."

Edmund was implying that King Lear and Cordelia would not get a fair trial although he already knew that the Duke of Albany was planning to pardon them.

The Duke of Albany said to him, "Sir, if you don't mind, I regard you only as a subordinate in this war, not as my equal."

Using the royal plural, Regan said, "We please to regard him as your equal. I think that you could have asked what we thought before you spoke so rudely to Edmund. He led our armies; he bore the authority of my Kingdom and represented me personally. His direct connection to me may well stand up so that he — my deputy — can call himself your equal."

"Not so fast," Goneril said. "Edmund exalts himself because of his own abilities and accomplishments — those mean more than any titles or status you can give him."

"Because he has been invested with my rights," Regan said, "he equals the best."

Goneril said, "The investment of your rights in him would be most complete if he should become your husband."

"Jesters often prove to be prophets," Regan said. "Words said in jest sometimes turn out to be true."

"Stop!" Goneril said. "That eye that told you he would be your husband can't see straight."

"Lady, I am not well," Regan said, "or else I would answer with very many and very angry words. General Edmund, take my soldiers, prisoners, inheritance. They are yours, as am I. The walls around my heart have fallen, and my heart is yours. The world will now witness that I make you here my lord and master."

"Do you mean to marry and enjoy him?" Goneril asked.

The Duke of Albany said to his wife, Goneril, "You don't want to let them alone so they can get married, but the lack of your good will is not enough to prevent them from being married."

He added, "You don't have the power to stop their marriage."

"Neither do you, lord," Edmund said.

"Half-blooded fellow — bastard — yes, I do have the power to stop your marriage to Regan," the Duke of Albany said.

Regan said to Edmund, "Let the drum strike up, and prove that my title is your title. Fight and defeat the Duke of Albany, and then marry me."

She wanted to be Queen of all Britain. For that to happen, the Duke of Albany needed to be dead.

"Wait," the Duke of Albany said. "Listen to my reason for stopping the marriage."

He had read the letter that the disguised Edgar had given to him, and he knew that Goneril wanted Edmund to kill him and marry her.

He said to Edmund, "I arrest you on the charge of capital treason, and I arrest in addition to you this gilded serpent who has been your accomplice and has — unwittingly — given me evidence with which to justify your arrest."

He then said to Regan, "As for your claim on Edmund as your fiancé, fair sister-in-law, I bar it in the interest of my wife, Goneril. She is sub-contracted to this lord. She is under contract to me, her husband, but she has made a sub-contract with Edmund for him to be her new husband. I, her husband, dissolve your engagement to Edmund. If you want to marry someone, marry me. My lady is bespoken for; she is engaged to marry Edmund."

"What a farce!" Goneril said. "What a performance!"

The Duke of Albany said, "You are armed, Edmund, Earl of Gloucester. You have a sword. Let the trumpet sound. If no one appears to prove upon your head in a trial by combat your heinous, manifest, and many treasons, there is my pledge."

He threw down his glove as a formal challenge to fight Edmund.

He added, "I'll prove it on your heart, before I taste bread, that you are nothing less than the traitor that I have here proclaimed you to be."

Regan said, "I am sick! Oh, I am sick!"

Goneril, who had poisoned her sister, thought, *If you don't feel sick, then I will never trust poison again.*

Edmund said, "There's my glove."

He threw down his glove to show that he accepted the Duke of Albany's challenge.

He said, "Anyone in the world who calls me a traitor lies like the villain he is. That is a direct lie, and I am bound by honor to fight him. Call that man with your trumpet. Against anyone who dares approach — him, you, anyone else — I will fight to firmly defend my truth and honor."

The Duke of Albany called, "We need a herald!"

Edmund called, "A herald! A herald!"

The Duke of Albany said to Edmund, "Trust only in your own strength and courage. Your soldiers, all of whom were levied in my name, have in my name taken their discharge."

Regan said, "My sickness grows worse."

The Duke of Albany ordered an attendant, "She is not well; take her to my tent.

Regan left, aided by an attendant.

A herald arrived.

The Duke of Albany said, "Come here, herald."

He gave the herald a piece of paper and said, "Let the trumpet sound, and read this out loud."

The captain said, "Sound, trumpet!"

The trumpet sounded.

The herald read out loud, "*If any man of quality or degree within the lists of the army maintains that Edmund, supposed Earl of Gloucester, is a manifest traitor, let him appear by the third sound of the trumpet. Edmund will fight boldly in his own defense.*"

Edmund shouted, "Sound!"

The trumpet sounded for the first time after the reading of the proclamation.

The herald shouted, "Again!"

The trumpet sounded for the second time.

The herald shouted, "Again!"

The trumpet sounded for the third time.

Another trumpet sounded in answer.

Preceded by a trumpeter, Edgar arrived. He was wearing armor, and his helmet obscured his face so that he could not be recognized.

The Duke of Albany ordered the herald, "Ask him his reason why he appears upon this call of the trumpet."

The herald asked, "Who are you? What are your name and your social rank? And why do you answer this present summons?"

Edgar replied, "Know that my name is lost; it has been gnawed bare by the tooth of treason as if worms had devoured it. Yet I am as noble as the adversary whom I have come to fight."

The Duke of Albany asked, "Who is that adversary?"

Edgar asked, "Who speaks for Edmund, Earl of Gloucester?"

Edmund answered, "I speak for myself. What do you have to say to me?"

"Draw your sword," Edgar replied, "so that, if my speech offends a noble heart, your arm and sword may do you justice. Here is my sword. Behold, the right to trial by combat is the privilege of my honors and Knighthood, my oath and loyalty, and my profession and religion. I am a Knight, and I have the right to challenge you and to have my challenge accepted. Despite your strength, youth, position, and eminence, despite your victorious sword and newly forged fortune, your valor and your heart, you are a traitor. You are false to your gods, your brother, and your father. You have conspired against this highly illustrious Prince, the Duke of Albany. And, from the extreme top of your head to the dust below your foot, you are a traitor — you are spotted like a venomous toad. If you deny these charges, then this sword, this arm, and my best spirits are determined to prove upon your heart that you lie."

"I have the right to refuse to fight anyone who is beneath me in social rank, so it would be prudent for me to ask you your name and confirm that you are a Knight," Edmund said, "but since your appearance looks so fair and warlike, and since your tongue shows some sign of education, I spurn and disdain to do what would safely and properly by the code of Knightly conduct delay this combat. I toss the charge of treason back to your head. The charge of treason you made against me is a lie, and I hate it like I hate Hell. That charge does not stick to me; it glances off and scarcely bruises me. But I will use my sword to open a passageway to your heart so the charge of treason can enter immediately and rest in your heart forever."

He then ordered, "Trumpets, speak!"

The trumpets sounded to announce the combat.

Edgar and Edmund fought, and Edgar mortally wounded Edmund, who fell to the ground.

The Duke of Albany sounded, "Spare him! Spare his life!"

He wanted Edmund to confess his sins and crimes.

Goneril said to Edmund, "This is treachery, Earl of Gloucester. By the law of arms, you were not bound to answer an unknown opponent. You have not been vanquished; you have been cheated and deceived."

The Duke of Albany said to her, "Shut your mouth, dame, or with this paper I shall stop it."

The paper was the letter that Goneril had written to Edmund asking that he murder the Duke of Albany so that they could be married. The letter mentioned vows that she and Edmund had made to each other.

The Duke of Albany said to Edmund, "Just a moment, sir."

He then showed the letter to Goneril and said, "You who are worse than any name I could call you, read your own evil letter."

She attempted to snatch the letter from his hand and tear it up but failed.

He said to her, "No tearing, lady. I perceive you recognize this letter."

He then gave the letter to Edmund. It had not been delivered because Edgar had killed the messenger, Oswald, so this was the first time Edmund was seeing the letter.

Goneril said to her husband, the Duke of Albany, "Suppose that I do recognize the letter, the laws are mine, not yours. Who can arraign me for it?"

She was reminding him that she was Queen and he was merely her consort. She could not be put on trial in a court because as Queen she had no peers.

"You are most monstrous!" the Duke of Albany said.

She had not admitted that she recognized the letter, so he asked her, "Do you recognize this letter?"

She replied, "Don't ask me what I know."

She exited.

The Duke of Albany ordered an attendant, "Go after her. She's desperate. Restrain her."

Edmund, having read the letter, said, "What you have charged me with, that I admit I have done, and more, much more. Time will reveal all that I have done. My evil deeds are in the past, and I am passing into the afterlife."

He then asked Edgar, who had not yet revealed his identity, "But who are you who have placed this fortune on me? If you are noble, I forgive you."

Edgar replied, "Let's exchange charity. If you forgive me for killing you, then I will forgive you for the evils you have done to me. I am no less in blood than you are, Edmund. If I am more, then the more you have wronged me."

He took off his helmet and said, "My name is Edgar, and I am your father's legitimate son. The gods are just, and of our vices that bring us pleasure the gods make instruments to plague us. My father begat you in a dark and vicious adulterous bed, and his adultery cost him his eyes."

Edmund said, "You have spoken rightly. What you have said is true. The Wheel of Fortune has come full circle. I started low on the Wheel of Fortune, then I was on top, and now I am here, lying in the dust."

The Duke of Albany said to Edgar, "I thought that your manner of walking did prophesy a worthy nobleness. I must embrace you. Let sorrow split my heart, if ever I hated you or your father! I have never hated either of you."

"Worthy Prince, I know it," Edgar replied.

"Where have you been hiding?" the Duke of Albany asked. "How have you learned about the miseries of your father?"

"By taking care of my father, my lord," Edgar replied. "Listen to a brief tale, and when it is told — oh, I wish that my heart would burst! I wanted to escape the proclamation of my death that closely followed me — we value our lives so sweetly that we are willing to suffer deathly pains every hour rather than die at once! — and so I changed into a madman's rags. I assumed a semblance that even the dogs hated, and in this disguise I met my father with his bleeding rings whose precious stones had been recently lost — he had been recently blinded. I became his guide, led him, begged for him, and saved him from despair. I never — this was a grievous fault! — revealed myself to him and told him that I was his son until approximately a half-hour ago, when I was armed to meet Edmund in combat. I was not sure of, though I was hoping for, this good and successful outcome. I asked his blessing, and from first to last told him about my pilgrimage, but his flawed and overstrained heart was sadly too weak to support his life as he felt great emotions! His heart stopped beating as he felt two extremes of passion: joy because he had found me, and grief because I had suffered. He welcomed death: He died smiling."

Edmund said, "This speech of yours has moved me, and shall perhaps do good, but speak on. You look as if you had something more to say."

People in this society believed that it was necessary to confess their sins before dying in order to go to Heaven. Edmund had admitted that he was a traitor, but now was a good time to tell the others about the note that he had given the captain after the battle. Edmund did not do that; perhaps he was trying to scam God with a fake repentance.

The Duke of Albany said to Edgar, "If what you have left to tell is more woeful than what you have already told, hold it inside yourself because I am almost ready to dissolve in tears after hearing what you have said so far."

Edgar said, "What I have said so far would have seemed the pinnacle of sadness to those who are not used to sorrow, but an additional sorrow I will mention will amplify by much more and exceed that pinnacle of sadness I have already mentioned.

"While I was loudly lamenting the death of my father, a man came over to us. He had seen me when I was in my disguise as a wretched man, and he had then shunned my abhorrent society, but finding out who it was who was enduring such grief, he threw his strong arms around my neck, and bellowed out his grief as if he would burst the Heavens. He threw himself on the body of my father. He told me the most piteous tale about King Lear and himself that any ear has ever heard. While he told this tale, his grief grew powerful and the strings of life began to crack. Then the trumpets sounded twice, and I left him there unconscious."

"Who was he?" the Duke of Albany asked.

"He was the Earl of Kent, sir, the banished Kent, who in disguise followed his King who was hostile to him, and he did his King service that was not fit to be done by a slave."

Carrying a bloody knife, a gentleman arrived and shouted, "Help! Help! Oh, help!"

Edgar asked, "What kind of help?"

"Speak, man," the Duke of Albany ordered.

Edgar asked, "Why are you carrying that bloody knife?"

The gentleman said, "It is hot! It is steaming! It came just now from the heart of — oh, she's dead!"

"Who is dead?" the Duke of Albany asked. "Speak, man!"

"Your lady, sir, your lady," the gentleman said. "Your wife, Goneril, is dead, and she has confessed that she poisoned her sister Regan."

Edmund said, "I was engaged to marry them both. All three of us now marry — join in death — in an instant."

Edgar looked up and said, "Here comes Kent."

The Duke of Albany ordered, "Produce the bodies of Goneril and Regan, whether they are alive or dead. This judgment of the Heavens, that makes us tremble, touches us not with pity. We tremble because of the justice of the gods, but because of the evilness of Goneril and Regan, we cannot pity either of their deaths."

A gentleman left to carry out the order.

Kent slowly and painfully walked over to them.

The Duke of Albany said, "Is this he? The time will not allow the complimentary formalities that good manners urge."

Kent said, "I am dying, and I have come to bid my King and master good night forever. Isn't King Lear here?"

"We have forgotten the great matter of the King's whereabouts!" the Duke of Albany said. "Speak, Edmund, where's the King? And where's Cordelia?"

Some attendants carried in the bodies of Goneril and Regan.

The Duke of Albany asked, "Do you see this sad spectacle, Kent?"

Kent asked, "Why has this sad thing happened?"

Edmund said, "I was beloved. One sister poisoned the other sister for my sake, and afterward she slew herself."

"That is true," the Duke of Albany said. "Cover their faces." An attendant covered the faces of the corpses.

Edmund said, "I pant for breath and life. I mean to do some good in my remaining moments, despite my own evil nature. Quickly send — don't waste time — someone to the castle because I wrote an order for the execution of King Lear and Cordelia. Hurry. Send someone in time to stop the execution."

The Duke of Albany ordered, "Run! Run! Oh, run!"

"Run to whom, my lord?" Edgar asked. "Who has the order to execute them? We must send a token of reprieve."

Edmund said, "Well thought out. Take my sword as that token and give it to the captain."

The Duke of Albany said, "Make haste, for your life."

Edgar took Edmund's sword and ran.

Edmund said, "The captain has a commission from your wife and me to hang Cordelia in the prison, and to lay the blame upon her own despair, and say that she destroyed herself and committed suicide."

The Duke of Albany said, "May the gods defend her!"

He then ordered, "Carry Edmund hence for awhile."

Two attendants carried Edmund away.

Now King Lear, carrying Cordelia, walked over to the Duke of Albany. Edgar and an officer followed King Lear.

King Lear cried, "Howl! Howl! Howl! Howl! Oh, you are men made of stones! Had I your tongues and eyes, I would use them so that Heaven's vault — the sky — would crack from the intensity of the sounds of mourning! She's gone forever! I know when one is dead, and when one lives. She's dead as earth. Lend me a looking glass. If her breath will mist or stain the mirror, why then she lives."

Kent asked, "Is this the promised end of the world? Is this Judgment Day?"

Edgar asked, "Or an image of that horror?"

The Duke of Albany said, "May the Heavens fall, and the Earth cease to exist!"

No mirror was immediately forthcoming, so King Lear held an imaginary feather under Cordelia's nose. He said, "This feather stirs; she lives! If that is true, it redeems all the sorrows that I have ever felt. Her being alive will make up for all the misfortunes that I have suffered."

The Earl of Kent knelt before King Lear and said, "Oh, my good master!"

King Lear, concerned only about Cordelia, replied, "Please, go away and leave me alone."

Edgar said, "He is noble Kent, your friend."

King Lear said, "A plague upon you — murderers, traitors all! I might have saved her; now she's gone forever! Cordelia! Cordelia! Stay a little while in the land of the living!"

He bent over and positioned an ear over her mouth and said, "What is it you are saying? Her voice was always soft, gentle, and low, an excellent thing in a woman. I killed the slave who was hanging you."

An officer who had been present said, "It is true, my lords. He did."

King Lear said, "Didn't I, fellow? I have seen the day when, with my good biting curved sword, I would have made them who oppressed her skip. I am old now, and the troubles of old age have ruined me as a swordsman."

He looked at the Earl of Kent and asked, "Who are you? My eyes are not the best. I'll recognize you soon."

Kent said to King Lear, "If Lady Fortune were to brag about two men whom she first loved and then hated, one of them each of us would behold."

King Lear said, "This is a miserable spectacle around us. Aren't you Kent?"

"I am him — your servant Kent," he replied.

Wanting to test King Lear's understanding, he asked, "Where is your servant Caius?"

Kent had used the name Caius when he was in disguise.

"Caius is a good fellow, I can tell you that," King Lear said. "In a fight, he'll strike, and quickly, too, but he's dead and rotten."

"No, my good lord. Caius is not dead," Kent said. "I am the very man —"

King Lear, in a state of shock, said, "I'll attend to you in a moment."

"— who, from the very beginning of your change of status and decline into decay, have followed your sad steps."

"You are welcome here," King Lear said.

"I am that man," Kent said. "No one else did that. Everything now is cheerless, dark, and deadly. Your eldest daughters have destroyed themselves, and in despair they are dead."

"Yes, I think so," King Lear replied in a distracted manner.

He still did not know that Kent was Caius.

The Duke of Albany said, "He does not know what he is saying, and it is in vain that we present ourselves to him."

"It is very vain," Edgar said.

A captain arrived and said, "Edmund is dead, my lord."

"His death is only a trifle here," the Duke of Albany replied.

He then said, "You lords and noble friends, know our intent. What comfort can come to this great decay of a man — King Lear — shall be given to him. As for us, for the duration of the life of this old majesty we will resign and give to him our absolute power."

He said to Edgar and Kent, "You shall again have your rights with extra rewards and titles as your honors have more than merited and deserved. All friends shall receive the wages of their virtue, and all foes shall receive the cup of what they deserve."

King Lear made a cry of mourning, and the Duke of Albany said, "Look at him!"

King Lear said, "And my poor fool — Cordelia — is hanged! No, no, no life! Why should a dog, a horse, a rat have life, and you have no breath at all? You will come no more — never, never, never, never, never!"

King Lear felt a sense of suffocation — *hysterica passio* — and said to an attendant, "Please, undo this button for me. Thank you, sir."

He looked at Cordelia and said, "Do you see this? Look at her — look, her lips! Look there! Look there!"

He died, thinking that he saw Cordelia breathing.

She did not breathe.

Edgar cried, 'He faints! My lord! My lord!"

Kent said, "Break, my heart. Please, break!"

Over King Lear's body, Edgar said, "Look up, my lord."

Kent said to him, "Vex not his ghost: Allow him to pass into the next world! He would much hate the man who would keep him alive a while longer to suffer and endure the rack of this tough world."

"He is gone, indeed," Edgar said. "He is dead."

"The wonder is that he endured so long," Kent said. "He lived long after he should have died."

The Duke of Albany said, "Carry the bodies away from here. Our immediate concern is public mourning for all."

He said to Kent and Edgar, "Friends of my soul, you two shall rule in this realm, and the wounded Kingdom sustain."

Kent replied, "I have a journey, sir, that I must soon take. My master calls me, and I must not say no to him."

Edgar said, "The weight of this sad time we must obey. We must speak what we feel, not what we ought to say. The oldest has borne the most; we who are young shall never see so much, nor live so long."

# Appendix A: About the Author

It was a dark and stormy night. Suddenly a cry rang out, and on a hot summer night in 1954, Josephine, wife of Carl Bruce, gave birth to a boy — me. Unfortunately, this young married couple allowed Reuben Saturday, Josephine's brother, to name their first-born. Reuben, aka "The Joker," decided that Bruce was a nice name, so he decided to name me Bruce Bruce. I have gone by my middle name — David — ever since.

Being named Bruce David Bruce hasn't been all bad. Bank tellers remember me very quickly, so I don't often have to show an ID. It can be fun in charades, also. When I was a counselor as a teenager at Camp Echoing Hills in Warsaw, Ohio, a fellow counselor gave the signs for "sounds like" and "two words," then she pointed to a bruise on her leg twice. Bruise Bruise? Oh yeah, Bruce Bruce is the answer!

Uncle Reuben, by the way, gave me a haircut when I was in kindergarten. He cut my hair short and shaved a small bald spot on the back of my head. My mother wouldn't let me go to school until the bald spot grew out again.

Of all my brothers and sisters (six in all), I am the only transplant to Athens, Ohio. I was born in Newark, Ohio, and have lived all around Southeastern Ohio. However, I moved to Athens to go to Ohio University and have never left.

At Ohio U, I never could make up my mind whether to major in English or Philosophy, so I got a Bachelor of Arts degree with a double major in both areas, then I added a Master of Arts degree in English and a Master of Arts in Philosophy. Yes, I have my MAMA degree.

Currently, and for a long time to come (I eat fruits and veggies), I am spending my retirement writing books such as *Nadia Comaneci: Perfect 10*, *The Funniest People in Dance*, *Homer's* Iliad: *A Retelling in Prose*, and *William Shakespeare's* Othello: *A Retelling in Prose*.

By the way, my sister Brenda Kennedy writes romances such as *A New Beginning* and *Shattered Dreams*.

# Appendix B: Some Books by David Bruce

**Retellings of a Classic Work of Literature**

Arden of Faversham: *A Retelling*

*Ben Jonson's* The Alchemist: *A Retelling*

*Ben Jonson's* The Arraignment, or Poetaster: *A Retelling*

*Ben Jonson's* Bartholomew Fair: *A Retelling*

*Ben Jonson's* The Case is Altered: *A Retelling*

*Ben Jonson's* Catiline's Conspiracy: *A Retelling*

*Ben Jonson's* The Devil is an Ass: *A Retelling*

*Ben Jonson's* Epicene: *A Retelling*

*Ben Jonson's* Every Man in His Humor: *A Retelling*

*Ben Jonson's* Every Man Out of His Humor: *A Retelling*

*Ben Jonson's* The Fountain of Self-Love, or Cynthia's Revels: *A Retelling*

*Ben Jonson's* The Magnetic Lady, or Humors Reconciled: *A Retelling*

*Ben Jonson's* The New Inn, or The Light Heart: *A Retelling*

*Ben Jonson's* Sejanus' Fall: *A Retelling*

*Ben Jonson's* The Staple of News: *A Retelling*

*Ben Jonson's* A Tale of a Tub: *A Retelling*

*Ben Jonson's* Volpone, or the Fox: *A Retelling*

*Christopher Marlowe's Complete Plays: Retellings*

*Christopher Marlowe's* Dido, Queen of Carthage: *A Retelling*

*Christopher Marlowe's* Doctor Faustus: *Retellings of the 1604 A-Text and of the 1616 B-Text*

*Christopher Marlowe's* Edward II: *A Retelling*

*Christopher Marlowe's* The Massacre at Paris: *A Retelling*

*Christopher Marlowe's* The Rich Jew of Malta: *A Retelling*

*Christopher Marlowe's* Tamburlaine, Parts 1 and 2: *Retellings*

*Dante's* Divine Comedy: *A Retelling in Prose*

*Dante's* Inferno: *A Retelling in Prose*

*Dante's* Purgatory: *A Retelling in Prose*

*Dante's* Paradise: *A Retelling in Prose*

The Famous Victories of Henry V: *A Retelling*

*From the* Iliad *to the* Odyssey: *A Retelling in Prose of Quintus of Smyrna's* Posthomerica

*George Chapman, Ben Jonson, and John Marston's* Eastward Ho! *A Retelling*

*George Peele's* The Arraignment of Paris: *A Retelling*

*George Peele's* The Battle of Alcazar: *A Retelling*

*George Peele's* David and Bathsheba, and the Tragedy of Absalom: *A Retelling*

*George Peele's* Edward I: *A Retelling*

*George Peele's* The Old Wives' Tale: *A Retelling*

George-a-Greene: *A Retelling*

*The History of King Leir: A Retelling*

*Homer's* Iliad: *A Retelling in Prose*

*Homer's* Odyssey: *A Retelling in Prose*

*J.W. Gent.'s* The Valiant Scot: *A Retelling*

*Jason and the Argonauts: A Retelling in Prose of Apollonius of Rhodes'* Argonautica

*John Ford: Eight Plays Translated into Modern English*

*John Ford's* The Broken Heart: *A Retelling*

*John Ford's* The Fancies, Chaste and Noble: *A Retelling*

*John Ford's* The Lady's Trial: *A Retelling*

*John Ford's* The Lover's Melancholy: *A Retelling*

*John Ford's* Love's Sacrifice: *A Retelling*

*John Ford's* Perkin Warbeck: *A Retelling*

*John Ford's* The Queen: *A Retelling*

*John Ford's* 'Tis Pity She's a Whore: *A Retelling*

*John Lyly's* Campaspe: *A Retelling*

*John Lyly's* Endymion, The Man in the Moon: *A Retelling*

*John Lyly's* Galatea: *A Retelling*

*John Lyly's* Love's Metamorphosis: *A Retelling*

*John Lyly's* Midas: *A Retelling*

*John Lyly's* Mother Bombie: *A Retelling*

*John Lyly's* Sappho and Phao: *A Retelling*

*John Lyly's* The Woman in the Moon: *A Retelling*

*John Webster's* The White Devil: *A Retelling*

King Edward III: *A Retelling*

Mankind: *A Medieval Morality Play* (A Retelling)

*Margaret Cavendish's* The Unnatural Tragedy: *A Retelling*

The Merry Devil of Edmonton: *A Retelling*

The Summoning of Everyman: *A Medieval Morality Play* (A Retelling)

*Robert Greene's* Friar Bacon and Friar Bungay: *A Retelling*

The Taming of a Shrew: *A Retelling*

*Tarlton's Jests: A Retelling*

*Thomas Middleton's* A Chaste Maid in Cheapside: *A Retelling*

*Thomas Middleton's* Women Beware Women: *A Retelling*

*Thomas Middleton and Thomas Dekker's* The Roaring Girl: *A Retelling*

*Thomas Middleton and William Rowley's* The Changeling: *A Retelling*

*The Trojan War and Its Aftermath: Four Ancient Epic Poems*

*Virgil's* Aeneid: *A Retelling in Prose*

*William Shakespeare's 5 Late Romances: Retellings in Prose*

*William Shakespeare's 10 Histories: Retellings in Prose*

*William Shakespeare's 11 Tragedies: Retellings in Prose*

*William Shakespeare's 12 Comedies: Retellings in Prose*

*William Shakespeare's 38 Plays: Retellings in Prose*

*William Shakespeare's* 1 Henry IV, aka Henry IV, Part 1: *A Retelling in Prose*
*William Shakespeare's* 2 Henry IV, aka Henry IV, Part 2: *A Retelling in Prose*
*William Shakespeare's* 1 Henry VI, aka Henry VI, Part 1: *A Retelling in Prose*
*William Shakespeare's* 2 Henry VI, aka Henry VI, Part 2: *A Retelling in Prose*
*William Shakespeare's* 3 Henry VI, aka Henry VI, Part 3: *A Retelling in Prose*
*William Shakespeare's* All's Well that Ends Well: *A Retelling in Prose*
*William Shakespeare's* Antony and Cleopatra: *A Retelling in Prose*
*William Shakespeare's* As You Like It: *A Retelling in Prose*
*William Shakespeare's* The Comedy of Errors: *A Retelling in Prose*
*William Shakespeare's* Coriolanus: *A Retelling in Prose*
*William Shakespeare's* Cymbeline: *A Retelling in Prose*
*William Shakespeare's* Hamlet: *A Retelling in Prose*
*William Shakespeare's* Henry V: *A Retelling in Prose*
*William Shakespeare's* Henry VIII: *A Retelling in Prose*
*William Shakespeare's* Julius Caesar: *A Retelling in Prose*
*William Shakespeare's* King John: *A Retelling in Prose*
*William Shakespeare's* King Lear: *A Retelling in Prose*
*William Shakespeare's* Love's Labor's Lost: *A Retelling in Prose*
*William Shakespeare's* Macbeth: *A Retelling in Prose*
*William Shakespeare's* Measure for Measure: *A Retelling in Prose*
*William Shakespeare's* The Merchant of Venice: *A Retelling in Prose*
*William Shakespeare's* The Merry Wives of Windsor: *A Retelling in Prose*
*William Shakespeare's* A Midsummer Night's Dream: *A Retelling in Prose*
*William Shakespeare's* Much Ado About Nothing: *A Retelling in Prose*
*William Shakespeare's* Othello: *A Retelling in Prose*
*William Shakespeare's* Pericles, Prince of Tyre: *A Retelling in Prose*
*William Shakespeare's* Richard II: *A Retelling in Prose*
*William Shakespeare's* Richard III: *A Retelling in Prose*
*William Shakespeare's* Romeo and Juliet: *A Retelling in Prose*
*William Shakespeare's* The Taming of the Shrew: *A Retelling in Prose*
*William Shakespeare's* The Tempest: *A Retelling in Prose*
*William Shakespeare's* Timon of Athens: *A Retelling in Prose*
*William Shakespeare's* Titus Andronicus: *A Retelling in Prose*
*William Shakespeare's* Troilus and Cressida: *A Retelling in Prose*
*William Shakespeare's* Twelfth Night: *A Retelling in Prose*
*William Shakespeare's* The Two Gentlemen of Verona: *A Retelling in Prose*
*William Shakespeare's* The Two Noble Kinsmen: *A Retelling in Prose*
*William Shakespeare's* The Winter's Tale: *A Retelling in Prose*